Persuade Deep

Sexy Stories Collection

VOLUME 37

11 EROTIC SHORT STORIES

PARKER HEIMANN

Persuade Deep/ Parker Heimann. -- 1st ed.
Xplicit Press, an imprint of TLM Media LLC

ISBN-13: 978-1-62327-568-6
ISBN-10: 1-62327-568-7
eISBN: 978-1-62327-618-8

Printed in the United States of America

CONTENTS

1 FOR THE RIGHT PRICE

Holly had the blues again. It wasn't a deep depression that she was experiencing. This was more like a temporary sadness. The sadness came and went with her line of work. She was a hard working woman, but having a steady line of work was always hard for her. You see, she was a freelancer. In order to make ends meet, Holly had to stay one step ahead at all times. That meant applying to as many open spots as she could, setting the right dates, and making sure she could satisfy her employers without any complaints. Having a set job took a while sometimes, especially with the failing economy. Still, with her determination and lack of bitter judgment, she was able to take the jobs giving to her with no complaint.

Some people who freelance are writers. Others are artists and creators, or have some sort of managerial skill. There were many things that people did to work while remaining independent, not getting attached to a company or one field. Holly's fate and lot was a little different. You see, Holly's freelancing work dealt with sex. She had to find slots that would fit her time schedule and the schedules of her clients, set up arrangements, and meet them in select spots. From there, she could do her work. The client would be satisfied and Holly would get paid. No big deal.

Now, before you assume that Holly was a prostitute, a whore, or even the more sanitary term, escort, she would probably want you to guess again. Holly didn't consider herself by any of those terms nor did she think that she was breaking any laws. She was a freelancer, pure and simple. Either she would post an ad outlining her specific qualities or someone would have an ad that she could reply to in order to get work. Sometimes it worked out, and sometimes it didn't. Simply put, that was the way the ball bounced.

The last time Holly tried to get work with her freelancing work, she got arrested. This is exactly how it happened and what happened afterward. First, Holly applied to an ad that specifically wanted a "call girl" for "legitimate work" making "decent, honest cash." Holly was used to this kind of wording in ads being a safe cover for really good freelancing work. So Holly called the number in the ad. She spoke to the client personally. She used the lingo that people in her work use in order to get to the square root of what the client really wanted. Once she could confirm that the client could use her services, she agreed to meet him in a secluded area. She thought that everything would work out, that they had communicated well, and that the man was going to have the greatest time of his life. Holly had come out of her car with the works – her best "fuck me" boots, her tightest red dress, and her sluttiest makeup that she could come up with – everything that was a part of her honest living and decent freelancing job. As she ruffled up her hair to look a little wilder, she knocked on the door of the place she knew the man would be inside of. She was greeted with the pleasant surprise of a beefy man in a blue uniform with a badge on the front left pocket. He wore a hat and even pulled out another badge from his wallet. Immediately, Holly was sure of what was going on. This misunderstanding had happened before. Holly was getting arrested.

"Freeze!" the man said. "You're going to jail."

Damn! Holly thought... the man is a cop.

"But wait, officer! I just came to speak to the nice man that I was going to do freelancing work for."

The cop rolled his eyes and scoffed loudly. "Um, yes. That man would be me, miss. Now please turn around and give me your hands. I'm going to read you your rights and then we'll be on our way."

As Holly turned around, she shook her

head. "But, officer, how do you know that the person you are trying to lock up is me?"

"You sent me pictures," the cop said. "Remember? You sent me very accurate pictures of how you looked and what you usually wear on your escapades. You also sent me a description of the things you would wear during our encounter. You don't remember?"

"Um.... No."

The cop reached into his pocket. "Well, I have the transcript folded up. Right here."

Holly scrunched up her nose. "Transcript? You don't have it on a clipboard or something? It's kind of unfortunate how you have it all folded up in your pocket. You might accidently get donut crumbs on it or something."

"Hey, watch it lady!"

Holly fell silent for a second. Damn! She thought to herself as she started to move her feet around and tap them. She always did that when she was nervous. Sometimes, her clients thought it was cute when she did it, usually because she was nervous about how much she was really going to like the encounter. On this moment, however, she was not feeling cute. But she knew the cop was checking her out as he was arresting her. She could feel his eyes pinpointed on her like a hawk.

"Well, officer," Holly went on, "do you think that you might be mistaken? I mean these pictures-"

"Look, lady," the cop said as he held pictures up to Holly's face, "I've got the pictures right here."

Holly looked closely on the pictures before pulling back and giving a nervous laugh. "Well, gee, hahahaha.... I guess they are me... sigh..."

"Yes, Ms. Holly Vegas. These pictures are you. Now, if you would please, let's step to the car and I will take you to the station, okay."

"But, wait... we don't have to go to the station."

The cop looked at Holly with a stone face as his hand was placed upon her arm with a firm grip. "Ms. Holly, are you trying to delay me?"

"Oh, I'm sorry. It's just that... the way you're holding me right now... you're so big and strong, and I'm so slender and frail. It's just that... well, I have a job to do and it's sad that I won't be able to do it for you."

"Ms. Holly, are you trying to blackmail me?"

"Are you trying to say you don't find me attractive?"

The cop froze for a moment before sighing. "Of course, Ms. Vegas. You're very attractive. Women like you are usually pretty attractive. That's how you're able to get work and find mind to do these types of things to you every time."

"I don't know," the woman said honestly. "You know, sometimes I look at mug shots online and I don't see a lot of woman as pretty as I am."

"I'm not talking about random crack and meth whores, Ms. Vegas. I'm talking about women like you that get away with doing these arranged dates for sexual favors. Women that fancy themselves to be high class and beautiful, using prostitution to feed your needy lifestyle."

Holly Vegas gasped in shock. "Prostitution?"

"Yes, Ms. Vegas. Prostitution."

Holly shook her head. "Officer, I will have you know that what I do is not prostitution!"

"No? What is it, then? Or rather, what would you call it?"

"What I do is called freelancing work. Nothing more and nothing less."

The cop shook his head. "I don't see it that way."

"No?"

"No."

"Why not?"

"Well, for one, miss... you're prostituting yourself. That means selling yourself for sex. You are giving up your body for the demands of making another person experience sexual pleasure through a sexual act. You are doing it because you require money to do such a thing. That is prostitution."

The woman shook her head. "Well, gee, I guess that according to you, everyone should be locked up."

Getting aggravated and annoyed, the cop hid some of his anger and displeasure. "Ms. Vegas, what on Earth are you trying to get at?"

"Well, Mr. Officer, no disrespect, but you're talking about prostitution."

"Yes. I am."

"Well, you are working for the police department."

"An honest day's work," the officer said.

"Yes, but you are allowing yourself to work for the service of the public and your superiors, right?"

"Well... yeah. That's what you call a job."

"But you are basically prostituting yourself for your job."

"Ms. Vegas, I don't know what you are trying to say or how you are trying to link my job or any job to prostitution, but this is not going to work."

Ms. Vegas looked up in thought for a few seconds before dropping her head low in the sad recognition of failing. "Damn!"

The cop held Ms. Vegas by the arm, hoping that she had accepted her fate now. He couldn't help but feel a little sorry for her. He could see that she was a working girl, and yes, she was very attractive, but what she was doing was against the law. It was bad for society.

"So... can I take you downtown now?"

"Can you!" Ms. Vegas got on her knees and started to nudge her head at the cop's cock and balls within his pants. She could immediately feel it leap up in attention.

"Hey! You know that is not what I meant, Ms. Vegas," the cop held the woman's head back.

Holly looked up into the cop's eyes with a fiery flare. Her mouth teased in a devilish smirk. "You haven't had any in a long time, have you?"

The cop looked at Holly in surprise. "What?"

"Your cock. It's been lonely. I can tell."

The cop laughed. "You can't tell that. Get real lady."

"Oh, yes." Holly smirked with delight. "I can tell, alright. It's quite obvious."

"You're full of shit, lady, and you know it."

Holly licked her lips. "I could make that dick so happy."

The cop looked a bit sad before he composed himself, trying to get the woman to stop. "Okay, okay, we've played around enough. I need to get you into the car and down to the station."

"It gets lonely, doesn't it baby."

The cop was caught in his tracks. He didn't know what to do. Should he pick the woman up, make her stand?

"All those lonely nights. Wanting and praying. Having to work the beat. Pick up women that you wish you could have sex with because you have a wife at home that can't stand to look at you. What's her problem? A big, beefy man like you in a cop uniform? Mmmm…"

The cop was definitely freaked out, without a question. Was this woman psychic or something? It was like she was seeing his family life. He didn't remember telling her that he was married, and he sure as hell didn't say that he hadn't gotten laid for a long time. Was it the way his cock leaped up automatically as soon as the woman brushed her head against it? Any warm blooded human male with an attraction to the female species would have done the same thing, right? What was it about his reaction or his psychic energy that was different?

"God!" the cop thought. This woman has to have something going on in her mind. She's got to be a witch, a hybrid or something fucking weird and out of this world.

"How long are you going to live, huh Harold? Until someone puts a gun in your head?"

"I didn't tell you my first name!" The cop was angry. The only thing the woman would have known was his last name, which was Thomas. There was no way that she would have had that information. "How did you know that? Did the guys at the station set me up for this? Are they paying you to pretend you're a prostitute? What the fuck is going on?"

"I just want to fuck, Harold. Is that so much to ask? And for the right price."

Harold sighed. The woman saw right through him. He really did want to fuck her bad. "Okay, what's the price?"

"My freedom. No strings attached. Caprice?"

"Um... do you mean capisce?"

"Whatever, Thomas. I ain't Italian and neither are you. Listen, babe. You fuck me, I get free. That's a good trade-off."

"Okay. Okay, I'll do it."

"Mmmm, that's what I wanted to hear, daddy! Now, let me think... I always wanted to be fucked in a cop car."

The man growled. "Lady, we can't fuck in there. There are cameras all over the car. I'll get fired as soon as they see the footage."

"There's no need to worry about that. I've got super powers. Look. We'll fuck in the car and I will completely wipe out the footage on the cameras."

Harold's eyes lifted up astonished. "Really? You could do that?"

"You saw how I saw right through you, right?"

Harold was honestly convinced at this point. This chick was a witch or an alien. "Alright, that's good. My fantasy was to always fuck a prostitute in my cop car, too."

"I'm not a prostitute!"

"Right.... I meant streetwalker, no! I mean freelancer."

"That's better. Stop forgetting. Now, please, sir knight... can you take me to your love machine?"

The cop guided the woman to his car. He was ready to get busy with her. Carrying her by her back, he slowly opened the rear car doors and placed his new fuck pal for the evening inside. Her helped to remove her shoes and even nicely took her earrings out.

"Wouldn't want those to get caught in anything," the cop said.

"You're so thoughtful," Holly responded.

The cop lunged over Holly and looked at her for a while. Holly could tell that he was nervous and afraid of upsetting her.

"So," the cop began, "you wouldn't mind if I removed your skirt and your thong, would you?"

"No, babe. Go right ahead."

With the green light, the cop went ahead and pulled down the woman's lower article of clothing. Right there, gaping in front of him, was her wet and warm pussy, ready to be taken.

"Wow," he said. "It looks really good, and it even smells clean too." Unlike my wife's rotten fish waiting at home, the cop thought. God! How much his wife had let herself go? Why did he work to stay in such good shape other than out of fear of looking like the other blobs he worked with?

"So it's clean. Ha-ha. Are you just going to stand over me and talk about the way I interior decorate my pussy?"

The cop felt a little embarrassed. "No! Of course not! I really want to have sex, it's just that... I haven't had sex in a long time, and I'm afraid that I will make myself look like a fool."

The woman rolled her eyes. "Baby. I'm offering myself to you. You aren't here to impress me. This is your pussy. Take it like a man and have it for yourself. Fuck me, literally. Who cares about my feelings?"

Flabbergasted by what he was hearing, the cop was having an internal war of morals. The woman was asking to be fucked, but he felt bad about fucking her. He honestly didn't feel as bad about cheating on his wife – she was a bitch, anyway. He only stayed married to her so that he would have something to come home to and not resort to drinking. He felt more bad about taking advantage of this woman, treating her like the prostitute he still had problems denying that she was... and here she was, this "freelancer", saying that her pussy was for the taking.

Just go for it, he thought.

"So, are you going to take off my top and fully strip me or am I going to be clothed this whole time?"

"No," the cop said simply as he took the woman's last articles of clothing off of her body. She was beautiful now, the way she laid so perfectly in the cop car, waiting to get fucked. He could smell her pretty cunt, fresh and wet. It was enticing him. He hadn't remembered smelling something that good since he first entered the police academy as a young man. Now, he would get a chance to have fun with fresh pussy again.

"Okay, copper," the woman said with a sly look in her face. "Bon appetite!"

And chow down, the cop did. First, before he got comfortable enough to pull his cock out of his cop pants, he pulled out his tongue and teased the woman's cunt lips. The woman giggled as she felt the tongue start to lick at her cunt. The cop had to laugh, too. There was indeed something funny about the whole fiasco. She was laying there, getting her pussy handled by his tongue as it started to speed up, licking deeper, and pushing in to get more of a taste. She tasted really sweet. The cop rubbed her hips. Wow! He thought, she fits perfectly in my hands. He wished that he could fuck her all night, and this tonguing was good foreplay.

"Mmm," the woman said with a moan, "Mr. Officer, you're so hot and kinky. I can't wait to have your cock in me."

That was enough encouragement for the cop to pull out his cock. Zipping down his pants, the cop flung his throbbing cock out of his underwear and moved over the woman. Immediately, he stuffed the head of his cock into the woman's vagina, going to town. He pushed into her deeply, and soon he was creating a steady and constant motion, pushing in and out, in and out. She was wet and hot, her tunnel seeming to be nice and smug. The cop felt like a snake nestled in her hole. He wanted more. He had to keep fucking until he got as deep as he could get.

"Ohhhh," the woman said as the cock went in deeper. "Harder... faster!"

The cop was good at obeying orders. He had probably learned that from cop school and continued it in his daily work. The cop was shoving the cock harder and faster into the woman's vagina, teasing it, making it melt and get really hot and wet. Her pussy walls seemed to be spreading. For a woman that had had a lot of sex, it didn't take much to turn the lady on. It took the cop back to his magic days with the ladies as he fucked the woman in and out, making her drip. Yep, he thought to himself. You've still got it, old man.

"Fuck me!" Holly demanded, even though the fucking she was already getting was plenty good. "Fuck me!... hard... ooohhh."

The cop continued to fuck Holly hard. He held her down, digging into her and feeling her trickle all over his dick, her words murmuring at times from the satisfaction and not even making any sense. It didn't matter to him. He could tell that he was pleasuring her, bringing her to heights she hadn't dreamed of, and making her cum. If he could achieve that, he was on the right track. He couldn't wait to see her orgasm, hoping that they would both climax at the same time.

"OH, daddy," the woman screamed as she was climaxing already. The man was shocked; surprised that he could feel her pouring so much. He assumed she had climaxed. What the hell! He thought, just keep fucking her till you finish. The cop felt like he could go all night or all week if he had to.

The cop dug into her, spanked her, and even pulled the woman's hair. He was going to get his payment's worth. If he was going to free this prostitute back into society to do her little "freelancing" work and do something illegal for a living, then fuck it, he was going to get his just desserts! He wanted to see if she was really the type that should be doing such a job. So far, she was excelling. Singing his praises in bed, moving against his thrusts to help him hit and penetrate the pussy even deeper... these were just a few things that probably made a prostitute continue to get costumers. The temptation did cross the cop's mind, but he had to stay focused here. Already, he was breaking a lot of rules and a lot of the law as well. No matter what, he had to do this. He had to fuck this woman, make her cum, and give her the satisfaction he was looking for. That way, he would be happy, she would be happy, and he would feel that he broke the law for a reasonable cause.

A sexy cause.

The man held his cock firm in the woman as he felt himself cumming, giving a loud moan as all the cum shot into her. God! It felt so good. He had never wanted something so much. He felt his excitement slowly going, as the cum leaked out. If only it could have lasted forever.

The two lovebirds stayed in the car, looking deep into each other's eyes as they held hands. God! The cop had never experienced something like that before. He felt like he could fly that moment, just like a bird freed from his cage.

"God!" the cop said, "you're beautiful."

"So are you, babe. But now, you better get back on your job."

The cop nodded. "You're right. I had better."

Pulling out of the cop car as she gathered her clothes, the woman dressed quickly before running off in her fuck me shoes and blowing kisses to the cop. "Ta ta, lover boy – call me."

The cop sat in awe, blushing before he got into the front seat of his cop car and drove off. There would be more work to get into. He was sure he had already netted some other prostitutes to lock up.

 ଓୄଓ

"Tell Thomas that we need him in our office now!"

"The captain needs to speak to Thomas!"

"Anyone know where Thomas is at?"

The entire office was in a loud commotion that Monday morning. No one in the inside of what was going on would reveal exactly what was happening. Everyone just knew that the officials had to speak to Officer Thomas. No matter if it was no one's business anyone. Besides, the captain was out on duty and had to handle some things. They said he had been pulling all-nighters for weeks.

"Bring that rock headed dolt to my office immediately!" the captain shouted again.

Suddenly, Thomas came into the place. He was still a little tired from a lack of sleep, but he was happy. He had been happy for quite a few weeks now, actually. Thomas had always been a good worker, but lately he had actually seemed to enjoy his job, whereas before he just seemed like some meaningless robot taking up space.

As Thomas came in through the door, one of the cop ladies gave Thomas a very scared but concerned look.

"Thomas, you are needed in the captain's room."

Thomas looked at the woman curiously. "What for?"

The woman shook her head. "Nobody knows."

Thomas followed orders. He walked to the room and looked in. The captain was sitting in the room.

"Thomas, come in here this instant!"

Feeling nervous after seeing the captain so angry, Thomas nearly asked what was wrong. He didn't have to, though. The captain had a TV player and a VCR in the room that he immediately started playing.

Thomas was shocked to see the video that he knew his captain would want him to account for. In the backseat, there was Thomas romancing some woman.

"Wait, but... what the... that's supposed to have been-"

"I don't want to hear it, Thomas." The captain shook his head. "You know, this is going in the papers. When your wife sees this... and your wonderful children... oh wow. You should be ashamed of yourself. You're kicked off the force."

Thomas looked his boss in the eyes. "Kicked off the force? Fuck that! I quit!"

The cop growled. "Don't expect any good recommendations from us when you're looking for a job!"

"You're just jealous, limp dick!" Thomas held up a middle finger. "Fuck you!"

The police captain gasped as Thomas walked out of the office.

Ex-Officer Harold Thomas didn't fret. He reached into his pocket and pulled out him phone. "Hmmm..." Going to his contact list, Thomas pressed for the letter H and scrolled to Holly's name.

2 DOMESTIC WIFE FUCKER

There are probably many people in the world who see life as a hard thing, a daily challenge with little comforts. Richard had never been one of those people. He had everything that his heart desired. Anything that money could buy, he could own. Richard could get planes, clothes, yachts, mansions, and girls. He could afford to take single women shopping, dress them up for his own entertainment and not even raise a brow. As the heir of a huge fortune as well as a businessman in his own right, Richard couldn't help but go for the fine things in life.

Richard was a plain-looking, kind of a quirky guy; he kept his hair short and always dressed up a bit too much for any occasion. The guy just couldn't get enough out of wearing a suit and a bow tie. In intellectual conversations, he always seemed a bit too into himself. It angered the guys but really turned on gold diggers and horny women.

Even with the luck that Richard had with women and money, Richard had his challenges and struggles. Limits were hard to come by, making it easy to go overboard with what he paid for. He never checked the bank account or wondered how much he should budget; Richard could care less. The man had travelled the world over several times by the time he reached twenty-four. The late nights spent with other rich people and servants in classy places bored him. Sometimes, he wondered if there was anything else he could do in his life that would be more tangible or fulfilling.

Richard got involved in a few activities to distract his hands from his wallet. With an occasional hike or trip to the beach, he tried to figure out how to balance frivolous-spending and debauchery-filled life. When the goal of clearing his mind from the rich tastes that constantly drove it to levels of insanity failed, he would find himself back in a cesspool of sex and booze.

If there was any place he could find solace from the outside world, it was probably Angela's. Angela had met Richard at a masquerade party years ago. Richard revealed his face and Angela revealed hers. From there, they felt an instant affinity. Neither of them would ever go as far as to say that there was chemistry or fireworks, but they hit it off well as friends and sexual partners.

Angela was a pretty woman. She had very fair skin and deep red hair. Her body was lean and healthy, and her eyes were always low as if she was amused by a secret joke. Her teeth were white and her lips quite full and soft. Richard loved to kiss them.

Their first night of passion had been intense. The masked sex was pretty good. Richard had come to the party as a gorilla while Angela had merely worn a Venetian gown and mask. After Angela had gotten her pussy dug out by the tall man in the gorilla outfit, she helped Richard get out of his hot costume. When they were completely undressed, they both had the best sex they had ever had in their lives. It was nothing weird, kinky, or even peculiar. Richard held her down and, in missionary position, rammed his cock into her until she climaxed with him.

Both of them held onto the memory, even after three years of sex that usually proved to be spectacular unless the both of them were not really in the mood for too much. Then again, on another calm night, they would have another great sex session. Pillows and blankets ended up being thrown on the floor as the two fuck friends calmed down hours later. Staying in Angela's mansion and spending the time in her bedroom for the rest of the evening, Richard rested his head against hers, holding her tight.

"You know what you should do, Richard," Angela started to tell him as she saw him slumped over a bottle of champagne. "I've told you this before, but I think it needs to be said again. I can tell you're in a state of depression. Look darling, you know and I know it's best that you focus on settling down. I think you're starting to become overly bored with this mindless life you're living."

Richard looked up to the woman with a chuckle. He straightened up in his seat, probably realizing how vulnerable he was looking to her, how weak. It made him uncomfortable as he felt like his manhood was threatened. "Oh? And I would assume that you are the woman that you think I should settle down with?"

She laughed. "No. Not a wild girl like me. But think about it, Richard. You've had all that you needed to taste of sex and beautiful girls in your life. Get a domesticated woman. Someone that your mother and father would have been proud of if they were still around."

Anytime Richard's parents were brought up, even casually, it struck a chord in his heart. They had been taken away from him so soon. "I have to be honest, Angela. I don't really know what kind of woman they would want me with."

They wouldn't have wanted Angela—that was something that Richard could have counted on. Angela was the type of woman who was first in line whenever an orgy started, especially one with wealthy and available bachelors. They were not only fuck buddies but drinking buddies as well.

"If you really think that such a lifestyle

would work for me, I guess I could humor the thought." Richard laughed. "But I've never thought that getting married would be the lifestyle for me, honestly. I would rather just fuck and find myself dead in a hotel some day from alcohol poisoning."

Angela shook her head. "You know you don't want that, darling. Think about it. You've only got one life to live. You're privileged beyond your wildest dreams. The things you could do with the remainder of your time on Earth are many. Share it with someone that means something to you."

"You mean something to me."

Angela laughed. "Yeah. A sexual partner that you can also be friends with. But a wife? No?"

It was on another night that Richard decided to push things a little further with Angela's ideas. Maybe test the waters a little bit. They had only been making out so far, not reaching sex as of yet. Angela had her hands against Richard's cock, rubbing it slowly as she moaned against his mouth. She wanted him to dig into her again, make him moan and get drenched in her juices.

"So let's say you were my wife."

Angela stared blankly into Richard's eyes at first but then found herself giggling. She couldn't help but laugh. "Wait a second, are you bringing up what we talked about a few weeks ago?"

"It was a good idea. But I just don't know how to get around the thought."

Angela shrugged. "I mean, you just meet a woman that you would really like as wife material. It's not that hard."

"You can help me train for it. Don't you think?"

Angela sighed before moving up a little further on the bed and spreading her legs. This evening she was wearing a little skirt that showcased her long legs and a buttoned-up top. She started to remove her top at first, exposing her beautiful breasts. Her skin was a smooth and light as milk. "Well, what is it that you're looking for in a wife? Let's start there."

"Well... it's kind of embarrassing," Richard smirked.

"Oh, yeah right. You? Embarrassed? You're the most confident man I know. A weird man, but pretty confident. I couldn't see you get embarrassed by something, little less a preference."

"Well... this is more than a preference. Kind of more like a turn on, or a fantasy."

Angela smiled as she brushed some hair from her shoulders, "I'm listening."

"Okay. So, when I was younger, sometimes my folks used to watch these shows. They were sitcom shows they said they grew up with."

"Go on."

"They were these old 1950s sitcoms. Like the black and white ones?"

Angela laughed. "Seriously?"

"Yeah. And the wives on those shows were always really attentive to the house. They would iron the guy's clothes, make their food, do chores, and were always really supportive of the husband."

Angela laughed. "Yeah. Pre-feminism era, you could say."

Richard sighed. "Come on, Angela. You know I'm not really the most-enlightened guy."

Angela shook her head with a grin. "I know, I know. Look, I'm kidding. I know you like to be the head honcho. I know all about those old sitcoms. I used to watch them growing up myself. That's just how a lot of wives were expected to be in the 1950s."

"Really?"

"Yeah. At least in the middle-class suburbia sense. The kind of life you and I are completely separated from. It was an expectation for a while to behave like that. Except, well, it's sort of an exaggeration. It's a fantasy. The perfect, ideal wife that is always there for her man and does whatever he expects of her. It's nothing embarrassing or anything to be ashamed of." Angela licked her lips. "In fact, it would be an honor to play a role like that for you."

Richard smiled. "I knew you wouldn't get offended."

"Of course not, babe. Now, you want me to change my name for you or anything?"

"No... Angela is perfect. It's the perfect wife name. Don't you think?"

"Fine. And you can act like you're just coming home, getting off of work. Just like the old shows."

Richard laughed. "Alright."

"Okay, honey. Why don't you start?"

Richard was impressed and had to smirk. He always liked a little role-play, but he had never tried it with Angela. Their sex had always been more straightforward. He had put Angela on a pedestal. He wouldn't have minded if he treated another girl like a domestic housewife, but this meant something a little more. This session would be way different than any game he had played before. That he was sure of.

"Hi, honey," Richard said. "I'm home."

Angela smiled as she spread her legs, slowly removing her skirt. "Why, hello dear. I've made you some dessert. I believe you'll like it, it's your favorite."

Richard's face was excited as his eyes widened, starting at Angela's lap. "My favorite, dear? What's that?"

"Pie, silly." Angela threw her skirt and panties to the floor. Her bare vagina was now visible and gaping.

"Pie? Gee willikers, honey, that sure is my favorite."

"Oh, I'm glad honey. You know I do so much to please you. Now come over here and eat your pie before it gets cold!"

Richard started to get undressed. He zipped off the pants he had on before removing his shirt and underwear. Now, only in his socks, he got onto the bed, rubbing his hands together as he looked at his new meal. "Mmm mm."

"Bon appetite," Angela said as her hand grabbed her sex partner's head, shoving it towards her pussy.

Richard's muffled words of delight could be heard between the woman's legs as he started to eat her out. Angela was starting to moan in no time. She could feel him teasing her cunt, starting to lick at it and suckle the juices that were dripping. He even held and grabbed her ass tight in his hands.

"Yes, that's it. Make sure you, ahhh, eat it all." Angela tried to compose herself as she put her legs over her lover's shoulders.

Richard continued to moan pleasurably as he ate into Angela. She always tasted so good to him. She only wanted more of her. Rubbing her legs down, he stuffed his nose against her lap as he tried to get as deep as he could inside of her. His cock was throbbing before he took one of his free hands and started to stroke himself.

"Yes, don't stop, baby," Angela moaned.

Richard only had to eat her pussy for a few minutes. He was hitting all of the right spots. Angela was twitching and squirming, enjoying the session. She wanted more. Richard continued to provide for her, holding her as tight as he could before she squirted over his mouth and face. His tongue was lined with her wetness and flavor.

Before long, Angela was shoving her pussy up and down against Richard's face, demanding more of him. His tongue reached and struggled, licking and slurping around the cunt walls. She had a great orgasm.

Richard shot a loose spud on the bed before slipping away from Angela, trying to wipe the sticky cum off of his fingers. "God, Angela, was I the husband or were you?"

Angela laughed as she looked at Richard, staring at him eye to eye. "Well, think about this. The fantasy of a wife, domesticated and loyal, always serving and pleasing his husband—it's a popular fantasy, a well-known one. Men like to feel important, in-charge and at the head of their household. At the same time, a woman is more likely to rule quite a few aspects of the home life behind the scenes. Well, at least in the context that we're thinking of now, say in an older time like the 1950s and 1960s."

Richard shook his head with a slight chuckle. "Do you really believe that?"

"I would say that there are probably many situations where the home life is just like that."

"Wow! Where did you get your information from?"

"Wife Life magazine."

"Oh God," Richard said with a scoffing laugh.

"Laugh all you want, Richard. But it's true. I've noticed it in many marriages even today, especially with older couples."

"Fuck a real marriage," Richard said. "I'd rather just pretend to be married."

"Pretend?"

"Yeah. It feels like way too much of a hassle. Besides, this is a good way for me to work through a fantasy I had never really explored before now. I have to thank you for helping me with the idea. I need to be going now."

Angela looked to Richard as she saw him starting to get dressed. "So when will I see you again?"

Richard zipped up his pants. "Come by

my mansion sometime in the spring. I'll have something for you." With that, Richard left.

"Ladies," a butler said as he greeted the waiting women in the downstairs den. "Thank you all for coming this evening. The master of the house will be down shortly."

Each of the women had a different facial expression. Some of them looked bored. Some looked excited and eager. None of them knew what to expect, really. They all had their sexiest clothes on but still looked elegant. With nightgowns, high heels, and faces that wore a healthy bit of makeup, they wanted to empress their new employer. Hopefully, the guy would end up being normal enough to get tasks done exactly as they were highlighted in the instructional video. They had all been assigned a video to watch. They were assured that the plans wouldn't deviate from what was outlined. Things, they were told, wouldn't get too outrageous. Their host was a gentleman.

They had all heard of him. This Richard guy was pretty wealthy and even gossiped about in circles to be a spectacular lover. Each of them hoped that the rumors would be proven correct.

"You've all been chosen for a reason," a voice said as the sound of carefully stepping feet started to come from the stairs.

All of the women looked towards the stair, which met the ground from an ascending spiral. Descending the set of stairs was Richard. The women saw the man for the first time. He would have been a bit plain looking if it were not for his well-designed suit, chrome watch, and necklace. His eyes stared at the women casually as he seemed to assess them individually. "You have heard of me, I'm sure. Welcome to my home and I'm glad that all of you could have made it."

The women smiled and nodded, offering their greetings.

"Now," Richard started, wanting to get to business as soon as possible. "I'm sure you all watched the instructional video that I put together. You all know exactly what I want and what I am looking for."

They all agreed loudly, nodding their heads.

"Good. So tonight will be our first session. Each of you has been assigned to a room and given specific duties. My butlers and maids have prepared your clothes according to the measurements we got from you. There are enough aprons, dresses, and household products for you all," Richard smiled. "Well, ladies, let's get started. I'll get ready myself. See you all in a few."

The women got up from their seats, making a little commotion as maids and butlers entered the room, guiding all of the women exactly where they needed to go.

Richard's hand gripped the doorknob

leading into one of the rooms and opened it. He wore a simple business suit with a tie and hat. "Hi, honey, I'm home!" he said as he peaked his head into the room.

Immediately, a clapping audience track was played by one of his butler's in the control room of the mansion. Richard had instructed that the tracks would be played appropriately in accordance to whatever room he was in.

The room was set up just like a living room from the 1950s. There was an old TV set and an old radio on opposite sides of the room. Black and white photos were all over the wall as they showed Richard fishing, kayaking, and even camping. There were also pictures of models wearing vintage housewife clothes all over the wall, some in the process of getting naked. Some of the models even had strange things inserted into them like metallic toys and fruit.

"Hello, dear," the woman of the room said as she stepped out of what looked like a kitchen. "Did you have a good day?"

Richard looked the woman up and down. She was very pretty, a beautiful black woman with dark brown skin and ruby lips. Her dark hair with highlights was held up in a bun as she wore a bright blue dress with a white apron on. Her feet were in shiny red high heels that matched her makeup.

"Yes, honey, I had a good day," Richard said accordingly, improvising his own script. "The secretary kept serving me pies all afternoon."

A laugh track sounded.

"That's nice, dear," the fake wife said nonchalantly. The woman walked up to Richard and took his hat and coat, placing it on a coat track. Grabbing his hand, she took him to the center of the room and started to disrobe. As she dropped the apron on the floor, she reached out in front of her, rested her hands on the coffee table, and bent over a bit, showcasing her ass.

"Yeah, but I'm still hungry." Richard started to undo his tie as he walked up behind the woman, rubbing her backside.

"I made you something really nice in the kitchen," the woman said as she felt Richard hike up her dress. She could feel his hands on her underwear. A moan escaped her lips as she felt him slap her on the ass.

"There'll be plenty of time to check all of that out," Richard said before taking his cock and slamming it into the woman's ass.

The woman moaned as she felt the cock go into her. The front of her skirt was invaded by Richard's hands as he started to finger her. As he fucked her doggy style, the woman leaned over the coffee table, taking the harsh fucking with pride. She gritted her teeth as Richard started to bang into her, leaving her dressed up enough to start his domestic wife fantasy off pretty well.

The women that Richard had hired weren't run of the mill prostitutes. These women were friends of friends, beautiful actresses and models that were used to improvisation and strange requests. Richard had some persuasive hookups that offered the ladies the prospect of a good job. All of the information they received about payment was true, though sex had been fairly hinted at. It was no big deal. That was how these things always went and clients had to be careful.

Many of the women were socialites in circles Richard was used to visiting, women who threw themselves at men like himself. He had recognized some of the women though he only knew them superficially or casually. This woman he was fucking now could well fit into that category. She had been a fuck buddy of his friend Paul. He had heard that she was pretty submissive in bed and let guys do whatever they wanted to her. Richard didn't doubt that—here, the woman was giving herself to Richard freely, offering her ass and taking his cock in without complaint. Richard couldn't help but to spank the ass a few times. It would wobble, nice and thick in his hand.

This woman was moaning pretty loudly even for someone getting fucked up the ass, Richard thought. She was pretty tight as well—the walls of her ass were a bit painful on his cock. Nevertheless, she felt good and her skin was smooth.

The woman continued to pant, shoving her ass against the rich man's cock. Soon, her wet cunt was drenching all of the coffee table magazines. Pencils and cups were falling to the ground. The woman was moaning to Richard's satisfaction.

"You... smell... like... secretary, dear," the woman said with gasps before she moaned again.

Her words turned Richard on even more, making him fuck her in the ass even harder. "Sorry, honey... it's just... good pie, I swear!"

It wasn't long before Richard was shooting a huge wad into the woman's ass, groaning loudly before pulling out.

"I think that was good birth control, baby," the woman said with a grin as she rose up from the coffee table. "Now why don't you go into the kitchen and get your meal?"

Richard pulled up his pants and retightened his tie. "Sure will. Now you just go on to the front of the house, your payment is waiting. See you next week."

The woman started towards the door as another audience track played with laughing and clapping. Richard sat on the couch to regain some strength. It wasn't long before he was horny again. He walked right into the kitchen.

Right on the table was blonde woman, nearly naked with the exception of red high heels. Her legs were spread and her hands grasped the sides of the table.

"Dinner's ready," the woman said as she looked up at Richard.

Richard didn't hesitate with this partner. He pulled off his tie and threw it to the ground, unbuttoning his shirt and pants. He was very hot now and he wanted to get completely naked. After throwing his boxers playfully in the woman's face, he bent down to peel off his socks. "Honey, no shoes on the dinner table."

The woman threw the boxers to the

ground as she leaned up and looked at her high heels. "Oh, how foolish of me." She peeled the heels off with her feet immediately, letting them drop to the ground.

Richard pulled himself up on the table and over the woman. With his strong hands, he held her down and looked in her eyes. His cock was already throbbing fiercely as he took a gander at her boobs, standing out there with hardened nipples.

The woman licked her lips. "Are you afraid to suck?"

"No way." Richard bent down, licking and suckling her nipples.

The woman moaned.

Richard stuffed a hand up the woman's cunt. It was so warm. It felt like it could shoot like a geyser at any moment. She was dripping all over the table. She must have been getting horny when she heard Richard going at it with his first wife in the pretend living room.

"I made this... uh... especially for you," the woman said as she puffed her breasts with her hands, helping Richard suckle them. Before long, her arms were wrapping around his back.

Richard took this as an invitation. With his hard cock, he stuffed himself into the woman, starting to fuck her pussy. She fit like a coat right over his cock. He wondered which one of them was really the meal, since her pussy was as hot as an oven. He felt like he could cover his cock in her for days and not have a problem with it.

"Uhhh!" The woman bent her head back as she started to get a pounding from her rich play husband.

"Yeah, that's it... take it." Richard started to fuck the woman, going as deep as he could with each thrust. "Take it, honey."

"Yes, dear," the woman said as she started to moan.

The sound tracks would applause and cheer at certain moments. Whenever the women screamed, the crowd went wild. Whenever they moaned really long and pronounced moans, the soundtracks would do a strange "aww" manner. Sometimes, when positions switched a little, there would be a loud "oooooo... ahhhhhh!" coming from the hidden speakers.

Throughout the audience soundtrack, Richard continued to fuck the woman proudly, stuffing his cock in her and spanking her. In a matter of a half an hour, they went from missionary to a little sitting and riding action, his strong hands supporting the woman's back from falling off the table.

"Ahhhh!" she said with a moan.

The smell of sex filled the room. All over, it seemed as if their hormones and sweat filled the room with a dominating, lingering aura.

"Fuck!" Richard exclaimed as he finally came into the woman. His sexual juice spiked into her like oil squirting.

"Oh yes..." the woman said before collapsing into Richard's arms. She was starting to calm down, sweat drenching her as her matted hair collected over her face. Damn, Richard thought, the woman looked like she had her energy drained out. She looked like she was ready to go to sleep.

Easing her on the table, Richard grabbed his clothes up from the floor and spoke to whoever was operating the sound room. "That's enough fun for today. Tell all the ladies I'll see them next week. So far, so good."

Turning to his last partner, Richard grinned. "Do you need to rest before you go?"

The woman nodded her head. "Yeah... that was great."

"Good. When you wake up, merely go to the front and your money will be waiting."

Richard walked out of the room. No attachments. That was the way he always liked things. So far, this was all working out in his favor.

Within a couple of weeks, Richard was already developing an idea of who his favorite "wives" were going to be. He had noticed some of the women didn't get into it as he wanted them to, seeming to only be in the deal for some easy money. He weeded out those individuals pretty quickly. Other women, like those that went the extra mile in wearing their wife clothes with jewelry and aprons or assuming chores in a believable way, got his full respect and a full-time job.

In a couple of months, some of the women were staying at the mansion and receiving a pension. They were getting fucked quite often on a daily basis, and even signed a contract where they wouldn't fuck anyone but their play husband, Richard. There were many other things guaranteed by that contract and many others, including a change of their last name to Richard's, performing certain labors around the house, and keeping a required set of clothing clean and fresh. It only took a year before Richard had about twenty women staying on his premise, fulfilling the life of a wife the way he specified it.

Along with the set women that he kept as officially employed wives, Richard would get special guests to be a part of what he called "The Richard Wife Fucker" show, namely, various celebrities and models who signed a strict confidentiality act. Richard's ties to Hollywood helped out in this opportunity and he always told his friends exactly what he was looking for- a great actress with a love for pretend and skills in making a make believe environment not only believable, but pleasurable.

Richard's wives performed their domestic duties well but the best duty Richard got out of them, of course, was the sex. There were women that liked backdoor sex often, women that liked to give oral, and women that loved intimate missionary sex. Richard also liked jokes as they kept the laugh tracks that played through the hidden speakers of the house more believable in his role-play fantasies. Every now and then, he'd through in some S&M with his more adventurous ladies, strapping them down and making them recite grocery lists or the pledge of allegiance. He wanted a patriotic wife, after all.

In about two years' time, after seeing what a success the operation was, a very cheerful woman signed a contract with Richard. They met privately in his den to discuss things.

As she sat in that chair opposite from Richard, he couldn't take his eyes off of this special lady. She had picked out a perfect little blue dress to entice him as well as some pretty gold earrings.

"Lovely spring weather we're having, isn't it?"

"Why, yes, it is." Richard looked her down again. He could tell that she knew how much he loved red high heels and it went so perfectly with her own red hair.

The woman extended a fair-toned hand towards Richard. "Thank you for this opportunity."

Richard shook it. "Welcome aboard, Angela."

As she stood up, Angela wiped the front of her dress to smooth it out a bit. "Where would you like me to wait for you?"

"Oh, you can wait for me in the bedroom. My real bedroom. You know where it is."

"Hmm... I'll be there." Angela smirked and winked before exiting the room.

Richard laughed. Before, he knew that

Angela would have scolded him and told him that this was not what she meant when she said he should look for a wife. Even so, he knew that she fully understood, especially now. Richard wasn't the type that could have attachments, at least not real ones, or ones involving such a silly, frivolous thing like a real marriage. No way, he didn't believe in it. There were many things he did believe in and value, though, where everyone could be their own boss and get paid at the same time. With contracts, payment arrangements, and friends with benefits, everyone could be happy. Those were things Richard could get behind, or in front of, literally.

3 MOB BROAD

The autumn months were always nippy in the Big City. Frigid winds blew down the streets and into the alleys.

Nighttime always brought an even colder chill. A sense of danger could strike at any time and crime was rampant during the late hours. Illegal businesses found their niche in clubs and bars hidden in basements and pool halls. Gambling claimed fools by more than a dime a minute. With such nocturnal comfort in the Big City, gangsters made their own way separate from the law. They lived under a code of loyalty that few were lucky or unfortunate enough to understand—violation of such a code could mean death.

Maria knew this well. She was a beautiful woman—raven black hair, beautiful brown doe eyes, and a soft, seductive red smile. She was wearing her best little business suit today. Her boss had gotten her a lot of those kinds of suits—a feminine top with a tie and some short skirts that showed her legs from the mid-thighs. Not a lot of girls dressed like she did—they would have found it too masculine to pull it off. Maria pulled it off perfectly, possessing a strong and vibrant personality with a sexy allure. She may have not been indoctrinated or a recognized member like the guys she spent her night hours with, but as a woman working around made men, she had her own work to put in as well.

As a bartender in a brothel downtown, Maria got the most respect out of any woman in the place. She laughed at the way the workers were hustled back and forth, hour by hour, into many of the rooms upstairs with strangers. It wasn't enough for her to just sell herself like that. Even if she didn't own the place, she needed something to make her feel respectable. There was no one who would doubt that her ability to make and serve drinks was a great attribute of hers.

She watched as yet another john got grabbed and pushed down the stairs by two gorilla-sized men. One of them was a guy she had grown up with. His name was Ricky, a guy who was feared even for having a low rank in his gang. He was a muscle man, making quite an efficient bouncer and bodyguard for the brothel's owner. He didn't take crap from anyone.

After bringing the guy downstairs, they probably took a minute or two to beat the daylights out of him. Luckily, he was still living—it was rare that Ricky or Danny really killed anyone. The guy would probably get the hint the next time he tried to shortchange the girls, ask for something too bizarre, or whatever the fuck that animal did.

"I hope you got insurance," Ricky laughed before punching another guy and throwing him out of the door.

Slamming the door, Ricky and Danny dusted their hands off as they walked to the bar. They didn't look pissed off or irritated. In fact, they were smiling and laughing a bit. Danny pulled out a cigar and stood next to Ricky as Ricky pulled a seat and sat down. There were only three other patrons at the bar: two possible johns and one of the lady workers. They were looking down at their drinks and avoiding any unwanted attention from the big guys there.

"Damn guy thinks we got pooper shoots and not prostitutes," Danny said with a snarl. "Damn the bastard."

"Should've kicked his teeth out."

Maria had already prepared the guy's favorite drinks and placed them on a napkin with olives floating in them. She was pretty quick and well acquainted with what these guys needed after dishing out a good ass kicking.

"Maria, sure you don't want to work it upstairs?" Danny laughed.

"If I have to put up with crap like that," Maria said as she pointed to the door, referencing the john ejected from the bar, "then I would have to say thanks but no thanks."

"Yeah," Danny laughed. "You know I'm just kidding. But you also know you're pretty enough to do it. The dark hair and the soft brown eyes."

"Cool it, Danny," Ricky snarled. "That's the boss's girl. And she's like a sister to me." Ricky downed his glass. "Just keep the drinks coming, Maria."

Danny turned his head to the side with a sighing frown. "Jeez. No one takes jokes anymore..."

Maria picked up some of the dirty dishes off the counter. "You ladies work your problems out," Maria teased. Looking towards the stairs, Maria saw a disgruntled prostitute coming down. "Hey, you!"

The prostitute looked at the bartender, her angry expression swallowed by obedient nervousness quickly. "Yes... yes, Miss Maria?"

"You man the bar. I'll be right back."

The prostitute smiled as she walked behind the bar and looked at the bouncers. "Don't know if I can man the bar, but I can man the men around here."

Danny laughed. "Baby, I'll man you."

Taking the dishes to the backroom behind the bar, Maria walked over the sink and started running the water. It wasn't long before she heard the boss's voice sound out behind her.

"Hey doll."

Maria looked out to the man as she mixed soap with water, rubbing a rag over the dirty dishes. "Sammy boy, you come through the back again?"

Sam approached, loosening his tie and dusting the shoulders of his seat. "Well, I was hoping to come through the front this time," he said as he turned Maria to his direction, making her look at him eye to eye.

Little words were said after that as they began to kiss. Sammy pulled Maria close, turning off the faucet behind her before rubbing her back up and down, closing his eyes and inhaling her sweet scent in. Maria hugged him back, kissing deeply and leaning against him.

Sam pulled back for a second, pressing a hand down on Maria's breast. "So when are you going to suck my dick?"

Maria seemed a little taken aback, jokingly, as her eyes widened. She eyed Sammy up and down with a smirk. "Don't you mean to ask me if you can eat me out again?"

Sam looked to the left and to the right cautiously before looking back at Maria. "Don't say that so loud. You know how the guys would laugh at me if they knew about that."

"What are you so worried about? You like it." Maria shoved a hand under the bottom of her skirt and hiked a leg up as she pulled her panties down to her knees.

The boss blushed. "Yeah babe. Yeah I do."

"So...."

"Can I eat you out now? Please?"

Maria patted him on the head. "Awww. Well, of course, you can, baby. Now chow down, lover boy."

Sam grabbed Maria by the hips and started to pull himself down.

Maria stroked a hand in his hair. "That's it, Sammy Baby."

Sammy immediately went to his duty, stuffing his head under Maria's skirt and starting to eat her out. She tasted so sweet and her lips were so juicy. There always had a sense of embarrassment when Sammy did this, but at the same time, he felt a strong sense of fulfillment. Even though he was the boss of a very powerful crime syndicate in the Big City, this was where he always felt he belonged—at the knees of a strong and powerful woman like Maria.

He was happy to see that his tongue was doing the trick. He could tell. Maria had gone from gripping his head to gripping the side of the sink and shoving her pussy clit against his lips. Her hair was cut short and in the shape of a heart; Sammy always thought it was pretty cute.

"Ohhh... don't stop," Maria said, trying to muffle her voice so that none of the clients at the bar would hear her.

The boss pressed his face so close against Maria. He had loved her ever since he met her. He had fucked a lot of dames, but Maria was a firecracker. She took control without effort. That's what he liked about her—she had such cool eyes and such a composed posture, but when it came to work, she had to be the most alpha female he had met. That was why he gave himself so easily to her, submitting to her needs.

"Err... Yeah, eat it boy." Maria pressed the cunt into his face back and forth, soon bending her legs over his shoulders as his hands supported him. She let him dig into her cunt so smoothly with his tongue, feeling him lick every dripping drop as soon as it splashed near his tongue. Her ass cheeks clenched with each winning lick.

Sammy was throbbing in his pants. Maria's taste alone was enough to drive him wild. He reached a free hand down to his zipper.

"No, no," Maria said, protesting against Sammy's hand that obediently pulled away from the zipper. "You know the rules. No jerking until after dinnertime. Can't have you dropping your one minute load."

"Mmm...Mmmm," Sammy said in a muffled voice that Maria recognized as a "yes, dear." With that, there was no more talking during the chow session, only moaning and penetration. The tongue spun and curved until they achieved the goal they were hoping for—Maria's cunt spewing orgasmic juices into his face. He could always tell when he reached that final destination—Maria's legs would vibrate quicker as the juices poured out more than any other point of the lovemaking session. Then, without fail, Maria lifted up and pushed the boss away gently, leaving him with a dreamy smile on his face.

"I know you came in your pants," Maria said with a smile.

"I can't help it." The boss felt a rush of embarrassment. Sometimes he wished he could do more for Maria, but he was glad his tongue made up for his cursed stamina.

Maria hiked up her skirt before hearing a glass smash outside. She sighed as she heard Danny calling the prostitute behind the bar a clumsy bitch.

"Can't I leave anything alone for even a minute?" Maria started to walk towards the door.

"20 minutes, dear," Sammy said. "That's 20."

Maria went back to her business as Sammy headed upstairs to wash up and get another pair of underwear.

There were all sorts of headlines on Maria. No one knew it was her who was in a great deal of those news stories covered by the Big City Gazette, but it was her.

The funeral was shot up by a strange, mysterious woman in a mob suit, sitting at the back of a limousine that pulled away quickly. That was her. The boss of a rival hood gang that was assassinated right outside of his mansion. Maria was behind that one. Bodies of missing made men, anonymous threats to the police station, and even gun fights that took out suspected traitors and rats. Maria had handled a lot of work.

Her boss valued her. As a woman, and a beautiful one at that, it was easy for her to maneuver through places without suspicion.

No one thought of her as the type to get into trouble. She was too cute, too well dressed, and too seemingly innocent. Anyone that knew her well, however, wouldn't even dare to question the truth.

Ricky had taught her well: he had introduced her to the higher ups of the gang, given her gun lessons when they were still in high school, and taught her how to rob and steal. Here was this strong-arm guy who was also kind of noble in a way and respectable and who held up to his word. That's what Maria liked about him—his honesty and open heart, unlike Danny with his pride and idiocy that could be seen clean through a busted window. Maria always liked Ricky with his modest smile and trustworthy eyes.

"Sometimes I wish you wouldn't call me your sister," Maria said to Ricky as they sat in the quiet room in Sammy's mansion. It was right in the outskirts of the city. Sammy liked to live large and only shared his most intimate secrets with Maria. Since Sammy was out of town for the week on business, Maria took it upon herself to keep the place cozy.

Ricky sighed as he looked down at his polished shoes. "What can I say? We grew up together. I always want to make sure you're safe and I just have a lot of love for you. It's just...."

Maria shook her head. "You just want to keep it like this, don't you? Downplay your emotions... our emotions?"

Ricky shook his head. "Maybe we should

have thought about all this before I brought you to the gang. I don't know. I was dating that girl from uptown at the time. You always felt like family to me. Really, I'm not saying that just to hold you at arm's length."

Maria rolled her eyes. "Ricky, come on. You've always had feelings for me. You can't deny it. I can always tell when I look in your eyes."

Ricky looked straight at Maria. "We shouldn't talk about these things any further. The boss—"

"The boss lets me fuck whomever I want!" Maria slammed a foot on the floor fiercely.

It must have been quiet for 5 minutes before Ricky spoke again. "I've heard, you know? I know the boss lets you do anything you want. I wouldn't tell him I know, but I know. You fucked a lot of the guys, and you'll probably continue to. You may have the boss by the balls, but... I'm a man, Maria."

Maria couldn't help but pout.

"You've got to understand, Maria."

Maria got up from her chair, walking gracefully towards Ricky. She moved so slowly and gracefully like a cat as she placed her hands on his knees and leaned in towards his ear. "No, Ricky... you've got to understand."

Maria's hand zipped down Ricky's pants and pulled out his cock. She had seen it bulky in his pants, and though he denied it, she could tell how easily it went up whenever she was near. It was so huge and throbbing that Maria felt like she could pass out from the excitement. She had always wanted to see it, live in the flesh, and here it was, free from being clothed.

Maria looked into Ricky's eyes with saucy eyes squinted in tease as her face seemed so hungry for action. "What I need, Ricky, is a nice, big dick—a real dick."

"No PIs here, Maria," Ricky said, taking his last attempts to blow her off.

"Penile insertion, coming up," Maria said before she pulled down her panties and skirt past her high heels. She sat down immediately in Ricky's lap, lifting the head of his cock into her cunt and letting it slip in. No protection, just like how she liked it. It was amazing; she hadn't gotten pregnant yet. Well, how could Ricky know her secret? He didn't want to know. All he could tell was that as soon as she slipped that pussy onto his cock and got to riding, everything had felt so right. Her luscious dark hair was swinging, breasts coming out of her lifting top. Ricky lifted his hand behind her and undid her bra.

"Oooooh," Maria uttered loudly. She had to admit—this was a big dick. It was bigger than what she had imagined. She always thought Ricky was huge, but the thickness was a bit much. She almost wondered if she could really handle it. At the same time, she had wanted this for years, what seemed like it could have been lifetimes. She had to do this—it was a mob girl's duty to ensure the happiness of her boys, or so she liked to believe.

"Maria," Ricky said in a cracking voice so

soft that Maria couldn't tell if it was pleading to stop or pleading for more. She reasoned it was both. There was a look of regret in Ricky's eyes. She could tell he was fighting inside, feeling the need of resisting to Maria's charms. There was also a relief coming after years of trying to hide his sexual attraction to her. In this moment, he was getting his hidden fantasies fulfilled. How could there be any denial there?

Maria was fucking Ricky now. Her falling and rising motions had become harder and faster. There didn't seem like any sense in slowing down. They were united and one. Ricky wasn't surprised by Maria's need to be on top at all. He'd give it to her, let her have it, and allow her to dominate his dick all night long if she wanted to. Maria could feel Ricky's balls jiggle under her and slap against her ass at times from all the bouncing. Her cunt hadn't ever been this wide before, even when she had played with some dildos and other toy insertions Sammy had given her to replace what he couldn't do. Fuck it. She loved Sammy; Sammy knew that. But she loved Ricky too. She loved Jimmy, Joey, Louie, and all of the crew....

But she would never fuck Danny. No way in hell.

"Uggh..." Ricky said as he felt Maria pulling back over him, up and down. They were pouring in sweat now. They didn't know how much time had passed, but they were still at it, racing for orgasms and lost in the rhythmic flow. They were animalistic, moaning and groaning, yelling and screaming.

"Oh, Ricky," Maria said as she felt her cunt quivering. She forked up and down, up and down, just like a roller coaster ride. She went back in time to high school when Ricky had taken her out on a few dates back to the carnival. He was actually taking a chance back then. She really thought they would be sweethearts, but he held back. Now she was here, in his arms, over his legs, handling his cock and stuffing it deep inside of her. If only she could have this sweet moment always, at all times, and give more of her body for Ricky's pleasure. Damn, how could something so perfect be ruined like this?

Now, she would never be a onc-man girl. She'd always belong to the boss, and the boss would always secretly belong to her as her personal bitch. One thing that couldn't change, could never be won again, was a chance to be exclusive with Ricky. As much as she could dream of a life alone with him, nothing was alone with the mob, a lifestyle that both she and Ricky loved. It was bittersweet.

The shared orgasms were bittersweet too. So tasty. So thick and runny. They shared the juices with each other, suckling it up with their mouths and fingers. They had accomplished so much in the course of thirty minutes. They would probably rest for a moment and Ricky would be ready for round two.

Lying on the bed together, Maria strolled her hands through Ricky's now unkempt hair. "Now babe, was that so bad?"

"No, doll," Ricky said as he leaned in and kissed Maria on the cheek.

"Of course not."

In two minutes, they were at it again. Doggy style was next on the list.

"Hello?"

Maria was alone in the mansion with the butler. Walking away after he gave Maria the phone, the butler left the woman alone as she answered it.

On the other end was Sammy. "Maria, baby...been having fun while I was gone?"

"You know it," Maria said coldly, just the way Sam liked it. "Been having so many dicks to take care of the garage while you're out driving, babe."

Sammy chuckled. "You know I'm not as good at picking up drivers as you are."

"Oh? Being a big bad boss of a powerful organization should have its perks in getting pussy, babe."

"You know I love you too much to chase so much pussy around. I just wanted to know you were getting fucked."

Maria chuckled.

"I do have something to ask you, doll face. A favor."

Maria straightened up a bit. "A favor?"

"Yeah. Something really important came up. I need you to handle something for me."

Maria nodded. "Sure, babe. I can do that. Go on."

A car parked securely at an abandoned building in the downtown area. It was a Sunday, the only day the brothel was closed. People may have thought that the types like the ones Maria hung around wouldn't have any morals, but some things were more important than others.

Then again, the reason why the car was pulling up to this abandoned building was anything but innocent. Three guys were coming out of the car: Jimmy, Joey, and Danny. They had planned robberies in the building, done drugs, and fucked hookers. They actually kept the place up nice. Tonight would be a rather pleasant opportunity, one that only Danny had never gotten before—they were all going to have a special rendezvous with Maria.

"Guys," Danny said as he walked behind the two. "You don't know how long I've wanted to fuck the boss's broad."

"Calm down, Danny," Joe said as he looked at Danny with a bit of irritation. "Don't be so gaga. We've all fucked her before."

"It's great," Jimmy said.

"Yeah, it's great," Joe confirmed, "but the way Danny's acting, it's like the prick's never fucked a dame before."

Jimmy knocked on the door. They heard some feet shuffling from inside. There stood Maria, wearing only a towel over her cunt, her breasts topless as she looked at this suited men. Her eyes gave them the service already.

"So you guys ready to get it on in this filthy place or what?" Maria asked seductively.

"Yeah, doll," Jimmy said as he slapped Maria's ass and walked in with her. Joey walked in as well. Danny followed with a little more hesitation, some insecurity showing as he closed the door.

They walked down a small hallway and into a bedroom. Even though the walls looked like crap, the bed was of pretty big size. There were some holes in the room where rats had chewed in, bugs all over the place.

Danny folded his arms as he looked at Jimmy and Joe leading the girl to the bed. "Why couldn't we have fucked in the boss's mansion?"

Maria smiled. "You think you're man enough to sleep in Sammy's bed?"

Danny gritted his teeth. "From what I heard, yes."

Jimmy sighed. "Danny, would you shut up and just be happy with what we're getting here?" Jimmy bent down and kissed Maria on the stomach as Joe was already starting to get undressed.

"Oh yes," Maria said playfully as she felt Jimmy kiss up and down her torso.

Danny waited. He was a little afraid to join them so quickly. He didn't have the most confidence sexually—but damn he wanted Maria.

Everyone except Danny was undressed now, the other guys only in their socks. Jimmy still had his wife beater on, probably to hide his embarrassing beer gut. The boss's girl didn't care—she just wanted the dick. Maria was already reaching down and sucking Joe's cock. Jimmy had already reached behind her, grabbing her ass and slowly stuffing his cock into her. It wasn't long before Jimmy was ramming her. Jimmy even reached into her cunt from behind, pulling and digging into it with ruthless fingers, wanting to satisfy both holes. It surprised Danny how quickly Maria had started moaning, and he already felt like he was missing out.

"Oh!" Maria called. "Oh yeah! Hit it, guys. Hit it."

Danny swallowed a gulp.

Maria was between the guys, already getting handled like some old toy that could have come with the abandoned room. Danny had never seen her act so submissively, craving the dick, sucking on it, getting fucked from behind. It was such an overload on Danny's mind.

Danny had had it. He started stripping down to his boxers. He was hard but kind of ashamed to show himself naked in front of these other guys. Damn, he thought, "she's so hot." He pulled his cock out; why the hell was he holding back so? These guys were ramming her? When they were done, she probably would want to get much more. But what the hell could he do with her now? He thought about just stroking his cock until he could at least cum on her face. Fuck that, he would push Jimmy away and flip her over. He was so confused.

The guys kept fucking her... and fucking her... and fucking her.

Danny stopped thinking, trying to step out of his paranoia and worries. He walked up to Maria. Her mouth was so full of cock. He lifted up her face. Her eyes opened as she saw Danny's cock the moment Joey had already cummed into her mouth.

As Joey pulled his cock away, Maria slapped Danny's cock to the side before it could even reach two inches away from her lips. "Wait... you're... turn." Maria was so breathy and hot from getting fucked in the ass so hard. Joey had put a working on her face too; her jaws hurt.

Joey laughed as he stood nearby. "You're too slow, Danny."

Danny was a little enraged, his face red. "Wait a minute... why should I be waiting?"

"Cause... I'm in charge here," Maria said with some moaning forcing the words out. "Don't wanna... tell Sammy... you forced a turn."

"Whoa, whoa, babe," Danny said as he lifted his hands, his cock still hard and really wanting to fuck Maria's face. "No need to get the boss involved."

"Wait... your turn."

"Okay, okay," Danny said as he stepped back.

Jimmy continued to fuck Maria harder and harder. The speed was so fast. Danny had never fucked someone like that. He really wanted to prove himself to Maria. He could be a man, couldn't he?

Maria's sex juices were filling the air. God, Danny had never smelled anything that felt so good. Joey had already gotten dressed and walked out. If it was so good, why didn't he want to wait for round two? Whom was Danny kidding? He knew Joey was satisfied. Joey just wanted to bust a nut and he was able to do it. Now, if only Danny could get a taste.

He was jealous—jealous of the way Jimmy was making her moan from her ass. "Fucking her like a fucking pansy," Danny thought rudely. Danny felt like he had to prove his manhood—cum in her pussy, maybe even bake a cake to have as an heir to the boss's throne. Haha! Danny laughed in his sick head. Wouldn't that be a funny joke? The boss's kid would secretly be his. As he stared at Maria, it was hard to keep doing jokes though. Her face looked so exhausted. Jimmy was handling her well.

Jimmy squeezed into Maria with a final thrust and a loud "hrrrr..."—a funny noise to accompany a hilarious orgasmic facial expression. The gritted teeth, those eyes— Jimmy was done. He panted for a while, his motions stopped, before he slowly pulled out of the woman's ass. His cock was dripping, some of the spew sputtering over the bed. It smelled too. Danny didn't know how the lady could do it. He wanted to think of her as nothing but a common whore, a low down slut... but she wasn't. He couldn't even get himself to say that. She was more than that.

She was a boss.

Jimmy got up and grabbed his clothes, walking out. He didn't even bother to get dressed in the room right then and there. Danny looked on, shocked. He stepped up to Maria, watching her breathe heavily on the bed. He wanted her to say something, but she was just breathing there, huffing and puffing.

"So," Danny said.

Maria huffed. "So?"

"It's my turn, right?"

"Yeah," Maria said as she slowly lifted herself up, taking a seat. She spread her legs as she looked up at Danny. "You should eat my cunt."

Danny looked at Maria with shock. "What? Hell no, what are you, crazy?"

Maria laughed. "Oh... bet you'd like it if I sucked your cock."

"Well, yeah."

"Oh yeah... that would be a mind-blowing experience." Maria started to finger herself as she started to come a little closer.

Danny got really excited... until he saw the gun Maria produced from one of the pillows.

"Wait!"

It was too late. Maria had aimed at Danny's head and killed him instantly. She didn't really mind killing. It was kind of different and funny after sex, but hey, what could she say? The boss had called a hit. Sammy was tired of Danny disrespecting the girls. Business was business.

Jimmy and Joey came back in the room,

fully dressed. They already had gallons of bleach ready. "All the other tools are outside."

"Good. Clean up this mess. I got a date." Maria got up from the bed. "Ricky's driving me to pick up the boss. We got a dinner planned together, the three of us."

"We'll have everything cleaned up by the time you get back to the mansion."

"That's good. Don't bother meeting us there. See you at work."

Maria walked out of the room, letting the guys clean up the mess. Her work there was done. It was hard being a mob broad, but there was no one better at it.

4 MOB BROAD 2
Love Is Pain

It was the 1930s. On another windy night in the Big City, the taxicabs and cars drove around the late night blocks as, occasionally, characters in suits strolled with dolled-up women around their arms. This wasn't exactly the nicest part of the town. Police didn't stroll through these streets on a night watch, and you couldn't see a young officer on the beat or a patrol squadron car for miles. Cats pawed through trash for some leftovers, and wild dogs would bark and howl at the moon during different hours of the evening.

To some outsiders, they would consider this side of the town dead. The truth was the very opposite. This was the time period where the street became more alive than usual. As strong gusts of air breathed through each alleyway and intersection, kicking up old newspapers that paperboys had left behind, the rulers of the night were up to their antics. Night in the Big City belonged to the gangsters, the mob men of a classic era that was still painting its own mythological legacy.

In an upstairs room from one of the tenements, strange loud sounds could be heard. There was a pronounced whipping sound as if something soft like skin was being hit hard. Occasionally, one would hear moaning—or a scream that sounded like it was being held back for far too long. It was repetitive. Such a sound came from that room all the time, but no one ever called the cops or was brave enough to check it out. On this side of the town, people minded their own business and let the affairs that went on in closed doors remain private.

That particular room was a small apartment that was rented by Gregory O'Malley. Sweating profusely in his wife beater and boxers, he went about his craft with a passion. He considered himself an artist in many ways, though he considered his artistic pursuits to be a personal affair, not public. In public, he was a businessman and could often be seen in illegal gambling halls, collecting debts or making a way for new drug products to hit the street. Tonight was one of his nights off from work, allowing his artistic side to express itself.

"And how!" as they may have said back then. Gregory's hand kept moving back and forth between a bottle of beer and the handle of a whip. He would pick it up and go back to his partner for the evening, a bombshell Russian blonde that he had met at an upscale art gallery months ago. She had already become one of his favorite playmates. With her wrists and ankles strapped to a circular device, Gregory was already going to town on her. The woman was naturally beautiful with pale skin and a body quite tall and busty for a woman. She was still moaning as her stockings hugged her legs, her bare feet held tight by the bonds, with some blood already dripping down the heel and toes. Each red rivulet came from specially formed slash wounds from the whip that Gregory held. The woman's back, legs, and even arms had been sliced quite nicely.

Gregory liked it rough and he was glad that this woman liked it that way as well. Sometimes, the ladies would bow out quickly. They didn't like the thought of their beautiful porcelain skin ending up sliced up like steaks. Still, it wasn't as if it were really going to be that bad. It was a little pain and pleasure, Gregory and the woman Olga reasoned. They had both had experience in these secret ways of playing, so maybe that was why they fit so well. Most women that Gregory knew were kind of ignorant and prude to these ways of living anyway.

Gregory blamed the social constructs of his time for making most women skeptical and weary of harsh love. Most women wanted to settle down and have a fairy tale wedding. Gregory patterned himself to be a "no fairy tale" kind of guy—no prince charming or even a frog for that matter. If anything, he could consider himself a wolf, but fuck it—whatever it took to fuck hot dames and beat them on his consent. It let out a lot of frustration that came with the mobster turf. They were a breed amongst sheep, the very society they exploited and ruled from the underground like demons shunned by the light. He could never go to the goody two-shoes route and be molded into what he considered a "pansy" like the rest of the people he saw going to work every day and mowing the lawn.

Even though he would work hard to convince himself that there was a wide societal framework responsible for making people soft, he knew that was bullshit too. For a gangster, the conventional was always the enemy, sugarcoating everything and keeping the harder realities away from "good" citizens.

Gregory could never be good. Never.

"So what's it gonna be, toots?" Gregory asked his partner. "Another round?"

"Oh Gregory," the woman said playfully with a heavy, sexy voice. "You know I can always take another beating."

"You and I both, sister," Gregory smiled. "Well, easy for me to say, ain't it? I ain't the one taking the beating."

"Of course not, baby. Someone has to dish it out."

"Ain't it the truth," Gregory wiped his brow as he reached for his beer. "I swear stamina can run low for sex at times—even for a boozehound like me. With a whip, though, I feel like I could go for hours and hours. I'm a king! By the way, that extra playmate I was promised should be coming pretty soon."

"Ooooh," Olga perked up. "Where did you get her?"

"She's supposed to be a gift from the boys. I'm not complaining." He rubbed his forehead. "Probably some prostitute. I don't care."

"Well, neither do I." Olga shook in her bonds before grinning. "Mind if you undo me?"

Gregory laughed. "Already?"

"Yeah. Undo the bonds."

"You're fucking playing. Look, the lady's going to come anytime soon. I'm going to whip you more, and then I'm going to do her. Then, I'm really going to do you. This is all foreplay to me anyway."

"Well, okay, babe. I just didn't want to be greedy. That's all."

"Don't worry about it." Gregory walked up to Olga and held up her chin. Her nipples were so perky in the light of the room as her boobs bounced, all available for Gregory's taking. It made both of them hot. "As soon as she sees you here, all sexy and ripped up, bloody... she's bound to take a liking."

Olga looked into Gregory's eyes. "She doesn't know that we like it... painful?"

Gregory shrugged. "The guys told me they explained it to her, but you know how they can be. Hints that don't really reveal things too much, kind of half-lies. If the babe freaks as soon as she steps into the door, I can't really say that I would be too surprised."

"I'm surprised you've told your little mob buddies about our games."

Gregory snickered. "When you're in a brotherhood, there're no secrets, Olga."

"I guess we'll find out if she likes this when she gets here," Olga said. "I hope so. Could give me a rest... my back is killing me."

The knock sounded at the door.

Gregory rubbed his hands together. "Oh baby." He grinned as he started to walk towards it. "It's going to be a real howl tonight!"

Opening the door, Gregory's mouth almost dropped as he saw the woman behind it. She had wasted no time getting in some sexy lingerie. How was she even able to walk to the door without someone seeing her in the building? He wasn't really worried about that anyway. She was wearing all black with frills on her panties and top. The black matched her hair, long and flowing. On her shoulder was a bulky purse. She looked at Gregory with a slightly made-up face that wasn't overdone, thank god. She smiled from an angelic face, her eyes just as bright and loving.

"Hello, angel," Gregory said with a face that was almost swept of any communicative emotion. "What's your name?"

The woman started to invite herself in,

stepping past Gregory. "Maria. Nice place you got here. Not too crowded with crap. Simple."

"I'm a working man," Gregory said with a laugh. "Please. Have a seat."

Maria obeyed as the man had instructed. Seeing a chair close to the woman in bondage, Maria took a seat, sat her purse at her feet, and looked up at the blonde.

"Olga," the blonde woman said, introducing herself with a smile.

"Olga, huh?" Maria smiled. "Quite charmed. Never had met another woman when I've made my rounds."

Gregory had gone into the kitchen, coming back with a bottle of wine and three empty glasses. Maria grabbed one of the glasses and held it out as Gregory first poured wine for her, then for Olga, and finally for himself. He placed Olga's glass on the floor, only a few inches in front of her bloody feet.

"You're pretty, Maria," Gregory said before taking a sip. "What do you do?"

"I'm a bartender," Maria said. "I've been doing that line of work for years." Maria glanced up at Olga's jagged back of open wounds before looking back at Gregory. "Aren't you going to let her down so she can drink wine with us?"

Gregory laughed with a slight harmless scoff. "Don't worry about her, lady. She likes it up there. Don't you, dollface?"

Olga nodded. "Of course I do, Master Gregory."

Maria smirked.

Gregory held his wineglass up and took another sip. "I'm sure the guys have told you about me, right?"

"Oh yeah." Maria nodded. "You're a made guy."

"Damn right, I'm made. And I worked really hard at it too."

"I'm sure you did, bad boy. I like made guys."

Gregory smiled. He liked this girl's style. "You uh... got any experience with S&M?"

"S&M?"

"Yeah. Sadomasochism. Pleasure and pain. Things of that nature."

"Hmmm.... Interesting." Maria tapped a finger near her lips in thought. "I always wanted my man to beat me up, but he's too much of a sweetie pie."

Gregory looked a bit shocked, even worried. "You have a man?"

"Well, yeah."

"Does he know you're here?"

Maria chuckled. "Yeah. Of course he does. He gets off when I do things like this."

Gregory rubbed his hands together. He was starting to realize he was interrogating the woman a bit too much, but he couldn't help it. "So he likes you having sexual escapades with other people."

Maria shrugged. "Well... he feels he owes it to me since he's not all that much of a powerhouse in the sack, you know."

"I see." Gregory froze for a second as he tried to think of the next right words, spinning a finger in the air with needless fidgeting. "So is this a job for you?"

"A job for me?"

"Yeah. Like a prostitute. Are my guys paying you for this?"

Maria laughed. "No. No, I'm not a prostitute."

"Cause I can compensate you for this, you know. I'm just being careful. Lots of ladies aren't into this stuff, especially for their first time."

Maria rolled her eyes before smiling again. "I mean, I guess you could say I'm on a job. But I'm not looking for money."

Sighing, Gregory slapped his hands on his side. "All right, then. I guess we should get started." Standing up, he walked back to the table and picked up his whip. Pointing at Maria, Gregory winked. "You just sit there and watch for a while."

Gregory walked into his readying position. Seeing Olga already winching in anticipation before he even sprang into action, Gregory licked his lips. He always loves the beginning moments. His hand lifted the whip and let it crack, snapping against Olga's back. She wailed with a loud moan instantly, squirming. Another crack of the whip hit the woman on her back. She gave a yelp. The rhythm continued; blood starting to pour again as wounds reopened.

The sounds of the cracking whip filled the air as Maria sat calmly, lifting her glass and sipping it with a delicate hand. She brushed some of her dark hair from her eyes, watching the Russian maiden take the pain. Maria had to admit that the sight of this woman being beaten was pretty impressive.

She could see Olga's legs squirming, her limbs twitching, and her eyes closing as her mouth opened and let out gasps for breath and loud screams. Sometimes, Maria would catch the grinning wild face of Gregory as she stared over for a moment. It was a strange and interesting way of making love, Maria thought, but who was she to judge? She had done pretty kinky things herself, though she had never played with pain in such a way.

She would do it tonight. Anything to get the job done.

"Oh yes, god please, more master," Olga said with quick breaths. "I've been bad, please more." Suddenly, Olga's face got bright, her eyes wide open. "Wait, wait. Doctor... doctor... doctor!"

Gregory's whip stopped. The man was breathing heavily, the whip dropped to the ground. "What the hell? We just got started!"

Maria blinked as she looked back and forth at the two. "Will she be alright?"

Gregory nodded, shaking his sweaty head with a bit of disappointment. "Yeah. Yeah. Doctor is just our safe word." Gregory started to walk over to Olga, pulling out a key and starting to undo her bonds.

"Is it? I see." Maria shrugged. "I would think you would pick another word to make a 'safe word' less dramatic. Maybe something like 'banana' or maybe cucumber."

Gregory smirked. "That's a little too pristine for me, lady. What do I look like? A fruitcake?"

Maria crossed her legs as she made her voice raspy. "Oh... sorry to touch a nerve, cowboy."

After Olga was taken down from the circular contraption, she rubbed her ankles in her hands before massaging her wrists. Suddenly, she slapped Gregory in the face, her anger apparent as she shook a finger at him. "You should have stopped the first moment I said doctor!"

"Sorry," Gregory said sincerely, his drunken state showing. "I kind of got a bit too into it."

Olga folded her arms. "No matter. My turn is done. I'll get over it. Just remember it next time, please."

Gregory looked at Maria. "So... are you ready to give this thing a whirl?"

Maria stood up from her seat, offering it to Olga who took it willingly. Stepping forward, Maria undid her bra and threw it on the floor. "Yes. Shall we get started?" she asked as she stepped out of her panties.

"I would love to, yes." Gregory escorted Maria onto the contraption and locked her limbs in place. "Thank you."

Maria giggled. "No need for the manners, Greg. Just get to work and show me what this thing can do."

"Sure can do, lady." Gregory walked over to his whip and picked it up from the ground. It was waiting for him. He felt so much power whenever he grabbed it. He looked at Maria's back. This was going to be kind of hard. Her skin was so smooth, so soft, and so unspoiled. A part of him always hated to break a new girl in. "Are you sure you want to do this?"

"Ready when you are, doughboy," Maria teased.

SNAP! No sooner said than done did the whip crack against Maria's back. Its unexpected lash sent a sharp pain that seemed to vibrate through Maria's skin. There was no recovery time from the attack as one whiplash was followed by another, then another, becoming a pattern of slashing movements. Maria could feel gashes opening on her back. She had never felt anything like this before, though she had to admit that it was a little enjoyable. After holding her tongue for what seemed like seconds, she had to start moaning. She groaned a bit, even let out screams for the really painful hits. Her toes twitched as her eyes sometimes strained and shut, trying to tune on the intensity of the whipping. She was kind of glad that Gregory wasn't saying anything as he hit her—any dirty talk probably would have crept her out.

Olga sat in the chair with crossed legs, fingering herself with one hand and holding Maria's wineglass with another. As Olga sipped its final drops, she giggled. The blonde hadn't even touched her own wine yet.

Maria gritted her teeth, taking the abuse as long as she needed to.

Gregory stopped. Looking at Maria's back, he was impressed. This girl had integrity and endurance. "You're a tough cookie, Maria."

Maria heaved; her breath hot. Her body was sweaty but she was feeling it cooled down. "You're a bad boy, Gregory."

Gregory grinned. "Why, thank you. Anything for the ladies." Walking up to Maria, he threw the whip to the side of the room before reaching up for the woman's arms. He stared up to her, face-to-face, and reached up to kiss her. Undoing her bonds, Gregory smiled. "I think I've tortured you long enough. You're a natural, by the way."

Olga stood up and walked towards the two. "So I guess we'll have our little romp now?"

Gregory looked up to Olga as Maria stepped down. "Yes, I guess we will." He looked to Maria. "Maria?"

"Let's."

The three walked over to the bed on the other side of the room. Maria had her little purse along with her, putting it down on the ground nearby the bed. Maria could tell how much the little spank session had excited the two. Although her attention was first focused on Gregory, Maria was surprised when she saw Olga lunge over to her direction. The Russian kissed her with sweet lips, her hands pressed against her back with legs pressed against her legs. Maria was nervous about being kissed by a woman at first, but she had to admit that she liked it. The sensation was pretty good. Olga brought Maria down to the bed and hugged her tight as Gregory started to remove Olga's stockings. He watched the women go at it with their long kissing session while he undressed; he reasoned their passionate embrace to be good foreplay.

Maria rolled on top of Olga as they kissed, eyes closed as both of their hands teased each other's hair. Their nipples rubbed against each other, getting hard and perked up from the movements. Olga was truly a beautiful woman, and for a moment, it felt weird for Maria to feel her pussy pressed against Olga's. Neither one of them could enter each other. That didn't seem to be a problem for Gregory as he bent in front of Maria's ass and shoved a rather fat and impressive cock into her asshole. Maria moaned as she knelt on the bed. Olga crawled from under Maria, getting in a reasonable position to take her face and shove it in Maria's pussy. The blonde started eating the dark-haired beauty out instantly.

Both Gregory and Olga worked to handle Maria. For Gregory, it was easy in the back. He just held her and fucked her, feeling her asshole open more and more for his cock as he gripped her ass and held her as tight and in place as he could. Olga struggled a bit. Though she could eat Maria a bit, the fast movements from the doggy style made it difficult. Olga was accidently hit in the face at times, but that didn't deter her too much—she was focused. Her tongue would dig into Maria's cunt carefully, licking it with delicate licks, working to make the woman feel comfortable.

It worked. Maria was moaning, yelling, and asking for more. When the cunt eating proved to be difficult, Olga would go up to Maria's breasts, licking and suckling her nipples. Gregory continued to fuck her with little thought, digging into her ass, loving its strong grip. He could feel Maria's ass muscles as they flexed, and he wondered if she had gotten fucked in the ass often. He wanted to introduce her to pain more—her body was perfect for it. The markings on her back were already showing progress, and the thought of her becoming a doll for punishment really turned him on. Would she be an easy thrill to chase as Olga had proven to be? He really couldn't tell at this point. He didn't care why she was here—whether it was on business or to do a favor for his friends. All he knew was that he wanted to fuck her and whip her silly.

Maria screamed.

Gregory came.

Feeling his hot spud shoot into Maria's asshole felt pretty good, relieving him of his bewildered senses. As his rhythm slowed down, he saw Olga pull out from under Maria and give him a dirty, playful look. The gangster slowly moved the rhythm to a stop before pulling his cock out of the woman's ass. There was a drooling bit of pure white semen coming from his blowhole as the dick rose out of her. Yes, Gregory thought. This is heaven for a sadist.

Maria turned over and grinned, moving her hands in her hair and tossing it about wildly like a mad maenad. Then, almost without missing any beats, she looked over to Olga with a grin just as devilish as the one she gave Gregory before. "Now it's your turn."

Olga almost looked offended. "My turn? But you're the one getting broken in, not me."

Maria shook her head. "All ladies deserve to get their kicks. Especially tonight." Looking up to Gregory, Maria smiled. "I'm not a selfish taker. You get another round with Olga."

Gregory panted with an amused grin. "So soon?"

"Awww. The night is young, made guy. Don't tell me you're all tired now. Are you? Out of juice?"

Gregory snickered and sneered, "Who are you kidding, lady?" The mobster slapped his chest like Tarzan. "I'm the best. The fucking best! Don't you forget it."

Maria tapped her finger on her chin. She had had a lot of finger-tapping moments tonight. The two lovebirds amused her so. "Of course you are." Maria nodded her head over to Olga as she still looked at Gregory. "Think you can eat that fish for me, kitty cat?"

Gregory's face turned a bit angry now. "What do I look like? Some little bitch? Watch who you're talking to!"

Maria made a playfully pouty face. "Oh, don't be like that, lover boy. I won't tell if you won't."

Olga looked at Maria, then at Gregory.

"Yeah, what's with the hesitation? You think I'm going to taste gross or something?"

Gregory held his hands up in protest as he looked at Olga. "No, no, of course not, dollface! You know I love playing with you." He shook his head as he wiped the last traces of his cock spud on the bed's spread. "Okay, okay. So you want to see me eat her out? Fine, no big deal. I've eaten a pussy before."

Maria grinned wide. "See? I knew you could do it. You don't have to play big man for me, Romeo."

"Blow me." Gregory bent towards Olga's legs.

Maria watched as Gregory started to eat Olga. This was going pretty smoothly.

"Ohhh," Olga said as she took her hands and held Gregory's head, helping him. Her legs wrapped around his head, her calves resting over his shoulders.

Gregory's tongue moved up and down Olga's snatch and to the sides, eating it as if it were rice pudding. He had to admit—it tasted nice and clean, which surprised him. Olga was such a naughty girl. His tongue flicked and spun inside of her, trying to give her what pleasure he could. For his lack of expertise, he could already tell he was satisfying her. Both of their eyes were closed, their minds fixated on each other.

Maria had reached down to the side of the bed. She grabbed her purse and put it in her lap, rummaging through it.

Olga moaned. Her moans were very sensual, even beautiful. Gregory moaned and groaned between her legs as well. He wanted more of this. His hands rubbed up and down on the woman's thighs. If only he could get a better taste of her, he would go really deep. It seemed his tongue could only go so far. His macho mind mused on what a "lesbo" thing this was to do, but who cared? None of the guys could see him, none of his closest friends, those made men with huge egos. They didn't have to know any of this.

A shot sounded. A gunshot. It was loud and quick.

Jumping up, Gregory saw Olga's bleeding head. He screamed like a woman, leaping back as he saw that a gun wound had instantly peeled through the sides of Olga's skull. On the bed nearby still sat Maria, her face as jovial as it had been for most of the night.

"What did you do?" Gregory shouted. "What the fuck did you do? What the fuck did you do that for, you crazy bitch?"

"Shut up, Gregory O'Malley!" Maria stood up, a gun still in her hand. She pointed it in Gregory's direction.

Gregory had fallen on the floor. He started to crawl away as he looked up at this woman. What a kook, he thought. She must have been mad. Fucking nuts!

"You've fucked up, Gregory." Maria slowly followed the man, her gun drawn. "You've really fucked up this time."

Gregory was panting heavily, sweating more than he had during sex and the whippings combined. "What do you mean I fucked up?"

"The bosses, Greg. Your boss says so. My boss, who also happens to be my man, says so. You've fucked up. We don't like fuck-ups."

Gregory growled. "Get the fuck out of here. Dames don't have bosses. Who the fuck is your boss?"

"Sammy. Limp Pimp Sammy, as you put it. You know him."

Gregory shook his head as he held his hands up. "Wait, wait, you're his bitch? Is that it? No, no, wait, fucking forget this, bitch. You're crazy. I was only joking when I called Sammy that."

"He heard about it, Gregory." Maria was no longer smiling. Now she was getting pissed. "He heard what you said and it was way out of line. You don't disrespect a boss like that. Didn't you know the families were going to have a meeting soon after, Gregory? His family is an ally of your boss's family. You fucked up."

Gregory looked at the ground with disbelief. "You got to be kidding me."

Maria didn't laugh. Her face was still serious and her finger was still on the trigger, readying itself. "The Big City is a small town for made people like us, Greg."

Gregory laughed wildly. "Give me a fucking break. Sammy the clown is your boss? No fucking way! He sent a bitch to do me in? You're whacking me? Why couldn't he send his made guys to do it. I'll kill him. I'll kill him!"

"You won't kill anyone, Gregory."

Gregory looked up at Maria. "Well, you

have the gun. Didn't know sluts could be mobsters. Well, you got it now. You're gonna do me in, whore?"

Maria nodded. "Now that I told you your crime, I would be glad to."

The gun sounded. A bullet landed straight between Gregory's eyes, right on the forehead. The gangster fell instantly.

Maria slipped the gun into her purse. She didn't even bother to look down at the man another time. Having done what she needed to do, she got dressed, tidied up her hair a little, and walked out of the door.

All of that happened in the 1930s back in the Big City. It was one isolated event amongst many. Those were wilder times back then.

Present day.

The Gangster Museum of the Big City was always busy on the weekends. People flocked from all around to see many collectables and memorabilia from an older time. Statues, posters, guns, and car models lined the walls and shelves of the huge building. People from all over the world moved down the aisles, taking brochures and pamphlets as they tried to imagine just what the area could have been like in the seedy parts of the town back then.

"This," one of the tour guides said as she guided her group of about thirteen people to a statue, "is Maria Wise. Well, that was her main adopted alias anyway. Her first name was Maria, but her last name is a mystery for us, even today."

The statue was undeniably beautiful. The woman's face and eyes were so clear and soft. She wore a mobster suit that people were used to seeing on men but it complimented her figure so well. In her hat was a feather and in her mouth was a cigar. She held a Tommy gun in an aggressive stance so convincing that the statue could come alive, blow everyone away, and let not one person be surprised.

"She's often called the Mother Saint of Mobsters by some gangsters. Maria was one of the first women to get enough respect from the mob and get seen as a recognizable member. In fact, she was so respected that she was often sent out to do assassination jobs."

"What happened to her?" an old woman asked.

"Funny you should ask that. The thing is no one knows what happened to her. According to some documents, a lot of law enforcement agencies tried to communicate with her in order to bring down the mob. They felt that since she was a woman, she would be more willing to comply and give up evidence of illegal dealings. They soon learned that Maria didn't want to offer them any information. She stuck side by side with the mob and upheld a code of silence. In time, she disappeared—what happened to her, we're not exactly sure, but there are many theories that make speculations."

"What kind of speculations," asked a dorky man in glasses and a polo shirt.

"Well, the most popular one would be that she was assassinated—in a hit by either rival gang members, law enforcement men, or spiteful male members of her own gang. Another story indicates that she may have left the Big City and went into hiding. What the real story is that no one knows."

The tourists and visitors gathered around the statue, speaking amongst themselves and snapping pictures. After observing the statue, they followed the tour guide to the next exhibit. One person, however, stayed behind, looking the statue in the face as if it were all too familiar. Only after hearing a call on the museum's loudspeakers for the tourists to come back to the buses for lunch did the old woman bow her head and move on.

5 THE PERSUADER

Any first meeting with Misses Margaret Billingsworth left a weird impression on her guests. After having many curious businessmen, politicians, and other respectable figures come for visits, the word had gotten out that Margaret was quite unavailable. She was a strange character, an interesting heiress who possessed a hefty amount of land on the outskirts of the heartland. Her fields were covered with horses and cows. A small and loyal number of people worked for her, tending her crops, gathering her water from the wells, and keeping Billingsworth Manor clean. The place was undeniably majestic and it was hard to ignore the fact that the people working on her property consisted of only beautiful women.

They weren't necessarily women that you would automatically lump in with the models airbrushed on magazine covers or pacing catwalks in New York. These women, gorgeous as they were, had a country appeal of simplicity. They came from various towns that surrounded Margaret's land, many of the towns over 30 miles away. The wealthy woman had as much an eye for secrecy as she seemed to have for beautiful workers.

Anyone that had a chance to meet her would first wonder how she earned so much money. She denied that she had ever been a movie star or worked in entertainment for that matter. If asked about business practices, she would say that she knew nothing about a decent day's work a day in her life. If it was the have and have-nots, she would explain with a sense of reserve and modesty. According to Margaret, her fortunes came with the luck of inheritance.

"All of my fortune came from something my grandmother gave to my mother who gave the same thing to me," Margaret explained often.

When asked what that exact thing was, Margaret would always fall silent with a smile.

She was a beautiful woman. She looked like she could be in her forties, possibly, but she had looked this way for a few decades. Many rumored that she could have been in her eighties, possibly. Margaret must have had a good surgeon. She rode horses often but never participated in any races, keeping her livestock on her property with wooden gates surrounding the place. Besides the women that worked for her, she didn't seem to have any friends. Some would say that she was a sort of a wild duck, but what would anyone expect from someone so obviously wealthy? "Only the unfortunate had a chance to be normal," Margaret would say.

Her home's walls were graced with a variety of photographs and paintings. There were art pieces depicting her as she posed with her horses and her cows and in different rooms of her house. She had black and white pictures of her standing side by side with politicians alive and dead, going to balls, pavilions, and even city hall celebrations. Tall plants stood in flowerpots and vases in the corners, making each room more beautiful. There was always a woman tending to them, just like the women tending to the flowers in Margaret's gardens. For a woman that didn't have a working job, she ran her own home like a corporate operation. None of the women complained or protested. They were usually smiling, their eyes looking delightful as if they were in a permanent dream state, sleepwalking. They performed their tasks with high attention to detail. Everything had to be just right.

Everyone that worked on her property knew the drill – no one disturbed the Misses during her private romping. It didn't matter how loud the screaming got.

Someone was screaming quite loudly at this time of the day, which wasn't a surprise. These things were quite natural. A young woman's wailing was filling the halls, though muffled behind the Misses' big, heavy white doors decorated with vine-like patterns etched on its surface. Along with the screams came some loud electric guitar-driven rock music, played at a loud volume within the bedroom. Whether the music was played to cover up the intense screams or as background noise to accompany them, who knew for sure?

Inside of the bedroom, Margaret was having a private party. She had one woman sitting obediently, watching with her legs crossed in a chair. The woman's name was Veronica. She sipped on a cup of tea in one hand as her other hand held a small plate in the other. The cup would rest on the plate after a few sips. Veronica was dressed in a beautiful yellow summer dress with a matching hat and white gloves that the Misses had provided. She wore shades as well, pushing her dark hair to the side each time the tresses wandered in front of her eyes. Margaret liked it when an accompanying guest was dressed her best.

Margaret was the conductor of the show but she didn't need any costume. She was fully naked by now. Even her long and slim stockings had been thrown over the head of her bed. The covers and blankets were tossed about on the floor, the smell of cunt strong in the air. Margaret was moaning over her chosen worker for the day. Under her was a young woman named Rachel, screaming sensually yet loudly as she was being rammed constantly with Margaret's heavy dildo. The artificial cock was held in Margaret's right hand, pushing in and out harshly as Margaret licked her lips and teased Rachel's tits with her other hand.

Veronica couldn't help but moan as she felt her wet cunt under her dress. She really wanted to finger herself but, unfortunately, the Misses wouldn't allow it until after the session was done. Sometimes, out of some strange perversity, she wouldn't allow it at all.

Rachel's soft, peach-tanned body looked as beautiful as some pale skin showed on her naked ass. Her skin dripped with sweat and candle wax that was slowly hardening on her body. Sometimes, Margaret could be a bit rough and this was one of those times. Rachel's ass was already sore from an earlier round of strap-on sex. Her nipples were hard and still wearing drool from Margaret's wet lips.

"You're always so loud, Rachel," Margaret said casually as, suddenly, she pressed a button on the dildo. It was already vibrating with more ferocity. These toys always surprised Margaret. They hadn't been around in her time. Just when it seemed like sexual technology had reached its peak of ridiculous pleasure techniques, gadgets were the gift that kept on giving.

Rachel was moaning. Decades ago, Margaret would have had to lick the woman clean just to see her going into spasms half as well as this. Now, the women instantly entered the pleasure zone with a touch of a key. It could only get better.

Margaret could feel her hands dripping with Rachel's sex juices. Rachel got really wet whenever they got together – all of the sheets would end up completely soaked. As Margaret pushed in and out of the willing servant, she licked her lips in joy. She spun the dildo as she pushed it in and out of her fuck partner, trying to get as deep as she could possibly go. The music played loudly in the background, the guitars seeming to synchronize with Rachel's movements at times.

Veronica always thought that Rachel was a good catch for Margaret. She looked down at her legs as they kicked, Rachel's breasts heaving up and down with frantic breaths that could never catch themselves with nipples hardened in the lamplights. It was a shame that the servants could only play when Margaret told them to, Veronica thought at times, but it was Margaret that knew best. She just had that charm, that charisma, which could make a woman want to do anything. There was never any hesitation. As soon as Margaret looked at someone with those piercingly pale yet complex eyes, the servant would jump to do whatever made the Mistress happy.

As screams became prevalent once again, Rachel went in and out of different thought patterns. She wondered how she could have been convinced to do such weird and perverted things. Rachel had always been attracted to men. She never thought that she would end up working on a farmland for some old, eccentric woman with a hidden past. Most of the time, their initial meeting did seem to be a blur.

With another penetration into Rachel's

cunt, memories flashed back. There had been a political fair. Rachel was dating a young and promising candidate at the time. It was there that she had met Misses Margaret, the middle-aged "MILF" with well-kempt brownish gray hair, wearing a business suit with a campaign pin on the lapel. When Margaret had shaken the young woman's hand, she could felt something strange. The older woman's eyes looked into her, making her feel uncomfortable yet entranced at the same time. The grip was strong and a bit demanding. All Margaret said was hello.

Rachel had broken up with her boyfriend the next day. She said she had gotten a new job. He would end up losing the political race months later.

And a year later, Rachel would still be working for Misses Billingsworth.

Misses Margaret's powers of persuasion were so powerful and irresistible. She possessed other uncanny gifts as well. When she looked into a person and charmed them, it was as if she could know them immediately. Their thoughts, their feelings, and secrets were all revealed to her at the drop of a hat. That was why Rachel felt like Margaret knew her more than anyone else did. That, even more than just being under some unending spell of energetic control, was the main reason she knew she could never truly break away from Margaret. To run from someone that knew her better than she did herself was such a ridiculous thought. Rachel was sure that Veronica and all the other girls felt the same.

She was right under her, right where she liked to be. Her cunt was wet, soaking the surface of the bed as the dildo slipped inside of her. It hurt so much even though her boss had used many tools and toys on her before. She had probably hit her peak three times by now. It was labor-intensive but it felt so uncontrollably good that, honestly, Rachel couldn't demand an end.

As all good things came to an end, however, it did. With Margaret pulling the dildo out of Rachel, Rachel felt herself climax for the fourth time. She was left on the bed as Margaret got up to get her comb.

Rachel laid there, a sweaty mess, her hair disheveled and her body hot. She kept panting.

"Did that... please you, Misses Margaret?"

Margaret turned around as she combed her hair. "Hmm? Oh, yes. You can go now, Rachel. Make sure that you send Sarah in here and don't forget to prepare my dinner for tonight."

"Yes, Misses. Of course." Rachel stood up quickly, picking up a robe and pulling it on. She exited the room, closing the doors behind her.

Veronica sat obediently in her nice clothes, waiting for Margaret's orders.

"How did watching us go at it like that make you feel, Veronica?" Margaret asked nonchalantly as she wandered over to a cabinet in her room. She turned off the CD player on her sound system. The heat from her lovemaking session made her body drip in sweat. Picking up a little Asian style fan, she started to wave it in front of her face.

"I enjoyed it very much, Margaret."

Margaret nodded. "That's good. Maybe I should have it arranged that you enjoy Rachel yourself, huh, just the two of you?"

Veronica bowed her head. "Whatever you demand, Misses."

With a little chuckle, Margaret moved towards Veronica, holding the unfolded fan at her side, "Now, enough watching from you. I need more action." Leaning into her servant's face, Margaret brushed Veronica's dark hair away from her face as she leaned in and kissed her. Her tongue flipped into Veronica's mouth as if swimming, brushing against her tongue. A free hand held the servant's cheek as Veronica moaned.

Before long, Margaret dropped her fan to the floor. She placed her other hand in Veronica's lap, pressing against it as she kissed her. Veronica felt her temperature rising as she arched her feet, leaning back in her chair, wanting her mistress to take her then and there.

A knock sounded at the door.

"Yes?" Margaret said with a pleasant tone of her voice, turning away from Veronica's lips.

The responding voice answered back just as delightfully. "It's me, Misses. Sarah."

Margaret turned to Veronica and smiled.

"You may go now too, Veronica." Margaret said, "I want Sarah and to have some intimate time. We can play later."

"Oh, yes, of course Missus," Veronica answered without hesitation as she walked out of the room.

Margaret waited on the bed, her legs spread and open. "You can come in now, love."

Sarah stepped in. She was already naked, her clothes dropped at the front of the door. It was the command that Margaret had given her from the first moment she entered the house. "Always approach my quarters naked and willing." Many of the servant girls knew that command with little time spent on memorization. Sarah did just that without protest. Her sandy blonde hair was held up in a bun. Both of her legs were quite toned from all of the yard work she did during the day, her body sleek and her breasts bubbly.

Margaret looked directly into Sarah's face, her eyes flashing. Margaret didn't have to do too much to convince Sarah to do anything, but she loved charming the girls whenever she could. "Come, and close that door behind you."

Sarah closed the door, proud that Margaret chose her as a second matchup for the day. She had heard of the woman a long time before she had been claimed by her. There had been rumors in her town of a woman they suspected of being a witch, a demon, or something else – no one could quite put their fingers on it. All they knew was that there was a rich debutante that never aged, never courted anyone, and stayed isolated on her own large collection of land. These stories mainly stuck with the elderly, people that had lived in those old towns for a long time. With a newer generation of adults like Sarah, such stories were mere folktales their parents carried with them. That's what Sarah had thought before she met Margaret herself. All of those stories suddenly transformed into something real.

Living in the Billingsworth Manor had been Sarah's fate for the past two years. Now, she had her head pushed between Margaret's legs, licking her cunt passionately. Her tongue dug deeper as Margaret tossed her head with a moan, placing her fingers on the woman's blonde hair. It wasn't long before Sarah's bun was undone, the hair brushing against Margaret's legs. Sarah's hands hugged Margaret's ass cheeks as she rubbed her nose against her skin, feeling Margaret's already warm and wet snatch rubbing against her face.

Pulling up a bit, Sarah looked at Margaret. "You promised."

Margaret smiled. "You are a strong-willed one. Such a good memory. I'm surprised."

"I want to know." Sarah dived back into the pussy, licking deeply.

Moaning, Margaret leaned against the bed. "I guess I owe it to you since no one has ever really asked before. Probably because they don't care, given all the pleasures I give them. You, however, are special." Margaret's right hand cupped over the back of Sarah's head, pushing it closer to the snatch. "Well, I can assure you that I am no vampire. And I am certainly no witch – well, I wouldn't consider myself one."

Sarah moaned a bit before getting some room to speak again. "Well, what are you?"

"I come from a long line of women, Sarah. We have always gotten what we want. From men, women... I just prefer women."

Sarah continued to moan during her eating session. Margaret's pussy always stayed so warm and fresh, pulsing, as if always needing to be pleased. "You're beating around the bush, Misses."

"Easy for you to say." Margaret laughed. "The truth is, darling, I don't know quite what I am. If there is a word for it, I don't know. I guess my people are human in their own way. We have long life spans, longer than the average human. I don't know how many of us are out there, but since I don't like dick, I'm pretty sure that the bloodline that was passed down to me will end with me."

"I want to get back to my old life," Sarah said before moaning.

"Nonsense, you fool. You know you like it here." Margaret shoved her pussy into Sarah's face. She wouldn't hear any more of what the woman had to say. Maybe she gave Sarah a bit too much leeway. It wasn't her fault that Sarah didn't fully cooperate. Sure, Sarah followed orders, enjoyed the sex, and did what she was told – but for some reason, there was a part of Sarah's reasoning abilities that always questioned Margaret. It was that part of Sarah's mind that seemed immune to Margaret's charming abilities. Even so, usually after a good session of sex, Sarah would fall in line completely.

Margaret made some more room on the bed. Immediately, Sarah followed. Rearranging her position as Sarah continued to eat her out, Margaret laid down and found Sarah's pussy, starting to lick and push into it as well. It wasn't long before Sarah was moaning in Margaret's lap. They forked at each other's cunts, juices running down their chins and pouring onto the bed. After Margaret knew she had Sarah where she wanted her, she moved her graceful fingers to Sarah's ass. She inserted Sarah's backside with two fingers rudely, making the woman twitch in astonishment for a moment. Quickly picking up the pace in Margaret's cunt again, Sarah regained herself, continuing to lick and spin her tongue more profoundly. The sensations going on in her cunt were amazing, nearly unbearable.

Margaret's eyes glowed as she dug into Sarah. The servant always tasted so good to her. Sarah obviously wore the apple-scented lotion Margaret had given her, knowing the Misses always liked her women to wear the distinctive smells she assigned to them.

Both Margaret and Sarah were moaning, their faces buried in each other's laps like burrowing moles. The cunts were so slippery and moist, pouring down and pulsing, wanting more. Sarah's asshole was hurting from the force of fingers pulling in and out of it, but she enjoyed the sensation at the same time, sometimes pressing against the fingers. Her ass muscles squeezed in all of the action. She was always surprised that Margaret wanted to make love to her in such an intimate way now. The Misses must have really liked her. Usually, with the newer servants, it was all wild sex and debauchery. Sarah had gone through that as well – becoming a part in acts that she sometimes found demeaning and strange. She had been charmed into ménage à trois, dildo sessions, strap-on sex, and even spankings without any noticeable sexual activity. As much as she had enjoyed it all, she thought that a good one on one lick fest like this one was always her favorite.

Margaret had opened up to Sarah, probably more than she should. With each sexual encounter, she would slowly reveal more information. "This wasn't good," Margaret told herself. She would have to be wiser, wittier, and a bit more cautious.

"Yes," Sarah moaned. "Make me come."

At that very moment, both women came. They felt their juices pour more profusely before Margaret pulled away. They were panting. The evening sun was already starting to set outside of the heavily curtained windows.

"That's it for now," Margaret said before clearing her throat and watching Sarah rise towards the door. Usually turned on by the chase of breaking in a woman, Margaret had to admit that trying to break Sarah was frustrating. Even after years of having her work on her property, showering her with gifts, and making her perform in sexual acts that granted so much pleasure, the servant girl was too inquisitive. Why did Sarah want to know so much about Margaret and her past, what she was, or where she came from? Sarah's curiosity was unnerving to Margaret.

Margaret had perfected her talents for a long time. She wasn't a vampire. She wasn't a witch. All of those things were true. She was very much human. Still, the techniques that she had learned from her family as a means to survive were powerful ones, abilities that wouldn't sit right in the hands of normal individuals. It was those secrets that she had to keep guarded from her naïve servants. A charmer's life was a very special one. Very few people could follow such a path nor understand it.

Margaret stood up and looked at the mirror. Before her was a beautiful woman, one that lived off a wealthy inheritance and enjoyed luxuries that she was very happy to partake in. Still, looking into those eyes she had, the eyes of one blessed and cursed with a rare talent, always made her feel alone. In a house full of servants, she was still alienated and frightened, and she even felt unsure of her destiny from time to time. She didn't know what to expect or what the future held. Would it be an endless sea of sex and ownership until she died, never leaving the property? Her mother had settled here at the end of her life. Her grandmother and probably family members before her traveled, saw the world, and used their special family gift in a variety of scenarios. Here, in her opulent manor with horses, cows, and women, Margaret also felt a little trapped. This was the life she made for herself.

"Persuader."

The voice was not Margaret's own. She nearly thought it was in her head, but it was coming from a particular place in the room. Looking around, Margaret examined her surroundings carefully.

"That's exactly what you are," the voice said, this time very clearly and not in Margaret's head at all. "A persuader."

Margaret looked to her right, seeing something materialize before her. It didn't seem human. Its features were very dark, charcoal and jagged like burnt skin. Delightful eyes glowed with fire, as jagged teeth covered with grit seemed to smile somehow. The thing's arms were folded as it finally made itself known: a dirty little devil, pacing the room slowly as its tail dragged on the ground.

"Who are you?" Margaret asked as she watched the demonic thing move back and forth.

"All will be revealed," the being said. "You may not know me, but your blood knows me very well. I am the being your ancestors made a pact with."

Margaret looked at the strange thing. It was so ugly, hideous, and disgusting. She could hardly watch it. If she hadn't lived the unusual life she lived, she wouldn't have believed that such a thing would enter her room. "What are you here for?" The devil laughed as it stopped pacing. "One thing." The being held out its hand as something flashed into sight, floating over his palm. It was a slowly spinning hourglass, all of its sand resting on one end. "The time is up."

Margaret laughed. "Time? What time?"

The devil snarled. "The time that your family has had to play with powers beyond its comprehension. Your lustful days are over, tramp. Time to meet with your family."

"Wait!" Margaret said as she raised her hand. "This is all so strange. You came and appeared out of nowhere. Can't we talk about this?"

"No," the devil said. He raised his hands as if preparing to do a magic spell.

"Wait, please," Margaret said again. Her voice was very controlled in this situation, as if she didn't realize how perilous such a situation was. "I'm sure that you have been working so hard."

"A devil's work is never done, lass, and we are many."

"Well... such work should have a rest, somehow." Margaret's eyes were flashing gently.

The devil lowered his hands, looking up at the human with some curiosity. "What kind of rest?"

"Well," Margaret rubbed her hand against her chin, "I'm sure a little thing like you isn't such a hit with the ladies."

The devil sneered. "I do well with devil women."

"Ah. A bit too ugly for beautiful human babes, I'm sure."

The demon's eyes raised aghast, his anger rising. "What – just what are you trying to say, lady?"

Margaret shrugged. "I'm just trying to help you out." She smiled, starting to pace a little herself and looking away from the demon. There was no need to charm him more. She had him right where she wanted him. "I can tell that you aren't the main runner of the show. You're just a servant, yes? I doubt you even formed the contract that you came to collect on."

"Well – "

"I have many servants." Margaret stopped pacing, turning back to the demon and walking towards him bravely. "Servant girls of a variety of tastes, smells... smooth to the touch, soothing to the senses. I'm sure your cock would enjoy them." The devil could feel himself ensnared in the woman's charms. Still, he could not get away from this and he knew it. It all felt so good and he trusted the woman. "What do I have to do in order to enjoy these pleasures?"

"Well, you must sleep with my servants, whenever you want – under my supervision and guidance, of course. Oh. And you must also allow me to live forever and do as I please forever, remaining in the same sound physical state as I have been. Then you and I can have as much fun as we would like."

"I do not have the authority to change your contract."

"Oh, but of course you do," Margaret snickered. "You have all the power. You're the big, bad devil." She rubbed a finger on the devil's chest.

"Yes... yes, I am." He couldn't help but grin. "I'm sure I can get my boss to see it this way as well."

"Shall you partake in some of my sweets now?" Margaret asked.

"Well, well yes. Where are they?" The devil looked at the door.

Margaret grabbed the devil's chin and turned him towards her. "No, no, no... in order to get anyone else, you must go through me first."

The devil's eyes widened. "You? But you're... you're so old."

The woman's eyes flashed.

"Well... not that old," the devil reasoned.

"Of course not, baby." The woman tickled the demon's chin as she pulled him over with her towards the bed. She could already see his charcoaled cock throbbing on his body that was so dead to the touch. For a little fellow, the evil demon seemed to be packing a lot in weight and length. "Allow me to break you in."

Margaret threw her legs open, pulling the demon over her. She wanted to feel him penetrate her as she stared at him face to face. She needed this to be intimate, close, and personal. Although she had already charmed him, she knew that if she really wanted him to be loyal and faithful to her, she would have to take over his senses completely. It was always after her first sexual encounter with a person that she could completely win them over. In mind, body, and soul (if the demon had one), she would be able to own him completely. The demon's thoughts, feelings, past experiences, and secrets were unraveling for her, exposed.

The devil dug into the woman with a ferocious push, tugging at her cunt with excitement. He had lied about being able to snag devil women – even the evil females of the deep ignored his advances. He was still a virgin. This was a good opportunity for him to get what he had been looking for a long time. Protesting thoughts rose here and there. This woman was strange. How could a meager human like this convince him so easily that fucking her would be a good idea? The demon tried to shake these paranoid thoughts. This was what he came for, wasn't it? Sex. He needed it, craved it, and, soon, would get plenty of it.

As he felt that pussy hug over his cock and move so smoothly with each push, the devil smiled wide. How nice was it to know that he had finally gained what he wanted for so long? People always thought that the devils had it easy, so much fun with debauchery and wild flings. If only they knew....

Margaret was moaning. The cock was

pretty big, stretching her own and rocking hard into her. She was shocked. Feeling it was even more intense than how she thought the experience would be when she saw the dick for the first time. She didn't know that it would hurt this good. She pressed against the demon, holding him by his hips as she held her by hers. They were pressing together, becoming one, fucking in missionary at a fast pace. The demon's eyes were closed, his blood rushing in relief. Finally, pussy....

Rocking in and out of Margaret, the devil thought about all the women he would get to screw. He had observed the outside of the manor before he entered to gain Margaret's soul. Though he had been focused before, he memorized the faces and bodies of the woman he had seen before he materialized. He had even taken a sneak peak of Margaret's last love session. This was better than most of the delights in hell. He wanted to be here to break himself into more women and to feel their warmth, their wetness, and the smooth feel of their skin. He wanted to cum inside of each one of them and leave a part of himself in them. He wanted to –

The fucking had been intense for ten minutes or so. Margaret was moaning and screaming loudly. No music played. There was just the warmth of their bodies, the panting of their breath, the sweat, and the smell of sex everywhere. It was getting wild. Damn, the demon thought, this is so intense. How can I hang in there?

He came. His cum shot out of his cock in

huge squirts. Margaret felt cum move inside of her as she smiled.

"Mmmm, demon cum," Margaret said before pushing the demon off of her playfully.

The demon panted on the bed as he watched Margaret get up. "Ohh, wow, that felt good. Now I can play with more?"

"Oh yes, you sure can. Don't you need a moment to rest?"

"No, no, no. I can keep on going."

"We'll see about that, big boy." Margaret moved towards a button on her wall and pressed it repeatedly. Before long, three new women walked through the door. As instructed a variety of times before, they were fully naked and ready. Their eyes were flashing, bodies glistening in the light.

"Devil," Margaret said playfully, not caring to know the demon's real name, "meet Stacy, Claire, and Ashley. Ladies, this demon wants to be your lover tonight."

The demon's eyes were fiery, his mouth watering in excitement.

Margaret leaned back on the bed with a smile. "He will not be getting his wish."

The demon's head shot up and looked at Margaret. "What?"

Margaret's eyes flashed bright.

The demon looked a bit sad. "But... did you lie? I... but why, mistress – "

"That's Misses. Misses Margaret. And you will ask no whys. You will only obey."

The demon looked blankly at the woman as she rose up from her bed.

"I have to tell you the truth, demon. Just

as I expect the truth from you. I'm very disappointed in you. Sure, the sex was great, but you break so easily." Margaret moved towards the mirror, idolizing her breasts in her hands as she puffed them up playfully. "I have a human girl that has a stronger willpower than you. I must admit I was excited to see something as supernatural as you existed. I've felt different all my life, even questioned my normality. Now, who cares? You don't impress me."

The demon hung his head like a scolded bastard.

Margaret smirked. "No one makes love to my women but me. You should have made that deduction as soon as you heard about me from your 'boss.'" The woman turned to the devil, smiling wickedly. "As a matter of fact, I am pretty sure that everything you told me about this little agreement, even your master, was a lie."

The devil's eyes opened wide. "Really? How could you be so sure?"

"Oh, really now." Margaret put her hands on her hips, walking back towards the bed with an authoritative confidence. "Because demons lie. That's what all the tales say. You are a funny one, demon. You saw a human woman with a special ability, but a human nonetheless. You reasoned me an easy one to fool. Underestimating my powers of persuasion was a big mishap – little did you know that my eyes can see right through your lies as well."

The demon looked down, ashamed. "I...

er... you're right, Misses."

"What are you really?" The demon sighed. "Just a wandering devil, madam. A meager, wandering devil with no real power. No real owner."

"Until now."

"Yes... until now."

"Good. Honesty isn't so hard, is it?" Margaret laughed. "Now, you, back to the bowels of wherever you came. Demon cock was a nice little experiment, but I must admit I'm a lover of cunt."

The demon looked disappointed. "Well... are you sure I couldn't please you more, Misses?"

"Well, you could by following my wishes exactly. I want you gone. Go to hell for all I care."

"Of course, whatever you demand." With that, the demon vanished in a cloud of smoke.

Seeing her pest problem was handled, Margaret smiled. She looked towards the naked girls awaiting orders. "Next."

END

6 AGRIPPA'S PUPIL

It was a fair spring weathered Sunday in Dole, France, and the year was 1512. The sun was shining and there were fresh breezes coming from the east. Most of the common people were attending churches throughout the country, paying their tithes and giving respects to their God. The choirs that filled the churches sent angelic voices that projected into the streets.

Some people couldn't afford to take a day off from their grueling occupations, not even for religion. Those diligent fellows were going about their daily work, unable to enjoy the fruits of the beautiful scenery. At the university, many students were studying just as hard as any other day, practicing their Latin script and reciting lessons in their heads, hoping to pass their exams. Professors were going about their lessons as well, preparing them for the next day.

There was one professor that was

probably doing things way different from most other people in Dole. Sitting in his study and compiling notes with scrolls and ink quills handy, Heinrich Cornelius Agrippa mused over some elaborate drawings. Many of the drawings portrayed astrological information, circles lined with signs, numbers, and Hebrew letters. There was a wrinkled scroll portraying a human male that was supposed to be a representation of the Universe, his torso's middle lined with planetary symbols, and Latin script. If most of the other professors and students saw pictures like these in the man's study, they would probably freak and consider the man a heretic. In fact, some colleagues and professors where already considering Agrippa a heretic without having seen any of his secret notes. From talks that he had given in classes, Agrippa had already painted himself as an eccentric, someone with interest in things that deviated from a pure, God-fearing society.

Let them judge, Agrippa reasoned to himself. The man had served in the military, undergoing experiences that only a former soldier could understand. He had excelled in the sciences and arts while studying as a student himself, ready to challenge anyone that would dare to debate him. Agrippa hated the academic environment sometimes. In a place that seemed to be geared towards intellectualism, learning, and sharing knowledge, the people that attended and taught in such places could surely seem ignorant and unintelligent. For this, Agrippa didn't blame religion; he, in fact, considered himself to be a fine and upstanding Christian with a focus on human compassion and justice. Still, it was an understatement to say that it didn't make him sick to look around and see the society that he was a part of. With the heavy hatred towards Jews that spread like wildfire throughout Europe as well as women accused as witches getting killed and burned at stakes, Agrippa wished that he could get away sometimes. Where would he go? He had built his own life in Germany, France, and surrounding countries. These lands were places that he knew well, where he could get work and continue to do his side passion, which was to study and practice the secret mysteries.

Agrippa had gained information from a variety of different cultures and traditions. There were the people of Chaldea with their time-honored religion of Zoroastrianism, peoples of Egypt and Greece with their ancient pagan traditions, and even the philosophies and mystical ways of the Stoics and Jewish rabbis. The professor had studied astrology as it had been learned in Babylon and other Middle Eastern countries. Even with all the man had learned, he was constantly studying, compiling notes and information that he could take to printing presses throughout the country. More than anything, even with his practical knowledge of using all this information, he mainly wanted to preserve ancient wisdom for generations to come.

It was hard to find a companion to share such information with. Agrippa had only had a few apprentices and even fewer colleagues down the years. Some people would come to him for knowledge, only to get freaked out by the realizations of how real magic was. Those individuals would end up running for the door, never to return. It was hard for Agrippa to relate to most people, and he noticed as he got older that he became more alienated. His love and pursuit for the secret arts would grow, and his ability to connect with normal people became harder to maintain. Sometimes, he thought about being a hermit, but he loved his family too much. He had a wife and kids in another city, constantly waiting for him to come back with the huge pensions he would make from the university, sometimes rivaling the amazing amount of money he made in the military. As much as he loved them and worked to provide for them, he even felt distant from his wife. He kept all of his arcane interests quite secret from her, only speaking to her as a lover and the mother of his children.

"God help me," Agrippa thought to himself as he looked down on his notes, scribbling away.

He remembered the one person he had connected with strongly. There was only one pupil that he felt a kinship so close that it defied words. With his other pupils, there were always conflicts, arguments in how magic and esoteric arts should be approached. With this one, however, there were no arguments, only magic. Agrippa wondered if he would ever get that again. Probably not. The pupil was gone, forever, though he did his best to keep her. There was nothing he could do but forget all that had happened and move on.

Still, he couldn't move on. His heart ached. Thinking of her face, her smile as she looked through notes with him, it could be too much. He even remembered when she performed her first spell and how surprised she had been when it went over well. As he sloppily tried to get through his notes, he would have to put down his quill at moments and just think. He would feel tears roll down his cheeks and suck in some wet dripping mucus from his nose, wiping his nostril tips with a handkerchief. He always got choked up when she came into his mind. What a horrible fate she suffered. Genevieve was her name. Sometimes he would just mummer it to keep her memory alive and still feel like her presence had a place in the world. Genevieve. Genevieve. Genevieve. He loved her in a way that he couldn't even relate to loving his wife. IF only he could have succeeded for her.

Never had the enigmatic magician thought that he would find his magical equal in the eyes of a prostitute.

Agrippa had met Genevieve four years ago on a rainy day in Cologne. He had just gotten back from a job with the military, quite happy as he had gained a huge amount of money. With plans to go back home and give some of his earnings to his family, he didn't think that there would be anything wrong with having a night of the town. Cologne had its little spots where a gentleman could go and get away from the heavy burdens of the world, places filled with loose women and alcohol. Although Agrippa was not a fan of drinking, he did like to remember that there were other women with different pussies ready for plucking in the world.

Agrippa went down a seedy block and checked out the sites. There was a number of peasant women that he could tell were new to the city, possibly women that got tired of the domestic life, widows and maidens that probably thought they would never be able to settle down. Why would they? The money was easy to come back and quick in these hidden pockets of Cologne. Agrippa couldn't blame them. If society hadn't been easier for a learned man of his stature and he had been born a woman in these troubling times, he would have probably joined the ladies in their need to sell themselves.

It wasn't long before Agrippa had run into a gentleman that he knew was selling women. He could just tell by the disposition of the man and the way he carried himself. The man had a hawk's eye as if he was looking for customers. His hair was a bit greasy and wet though his clothes were obviously new and well-kept for a person living in such a slummy area.

"Hello, sir, you there," Agrippa said as he approached the man. "I'm quite curious. How much are your ladies going for these days?"

The man shrugged. "I like to reason. Would you care to see them?"

After rubbing his chin in thought, Agrippa nodded. "Yes, I would like to. Show me the way."

The man took Agrippa from off the street and into a long hallway. As Agrippa kept up with him, he stared behind cautiously to make sure that this wasn't a set up. He had heard many stories of men being beaten up with their wallets stolen in situations like this.

Agrippa was relieved when the man opened a side door to one of the buildings and showed him a row of women, all waiting patiently. Some were already busy with customers who had their hands up their dresses and between their legs—they were taken, obviously. Agrippa still had seven to choose from, each of them offering something different. Most of the women were blondes except an extremely beautiful brunette, possibly an Italian. All of them were quite full figured and possessed enticing assets.

The pimp seemed a little annoyed even before Agrippa had been given a chance to look through them. "Alright then, sir. Pick one and then maybe we'll make a price, eh?"

Agrippa's eyes scrolled through the row of

women. God, they were beautiful. He could have his way with any of them. Part of him felt guilty but he always tried to be as respectable with the prostitutes as he could. As he looked through the line of women, he found his mouth watering. The dark-haired prostitute winked at him.

"Well?" the pimp asked impatiently. "Who will it be?"

Agrippa looked at the man with a bit of a scowl. "Would you mind giving me some time? You just got me here."

"Time is money," the man said.

Agrippa gritted his teeth angrily before trying to forget the man and looking again.

Walking closer to inspect the women, he was pleasantly surprised to see how healthy they looked for living on the streets. Their odor wasn't too much of a turn off and some of them even looked clean.

"Look man," the pimp said as he walked behind Agrippa, his face now raging, "you're wasting my time! Now are you going to purchase one of my girls or will you be making inspections of them all day?"

Agrippa looked to the man with disgust. "You really are impossible. I am disgusted and you have wasted my time. Good day." Agrippa started to walk out of the room.

The pimp growled behind the military man as he walked out, screaming and shouting obscenities. Agrippa didn't care. If he couldn't have a respectful transaction with the man, then there was no reason for them to communicate at all. He didn't care if he had the most beautiful prostitutes in the world. Agrippa would be able to find a worthy enough woman somewhere else.

Walking back onto the streets and avoiding the alleyways, Agrippa looked up and down the sides and near the slum houses, trying to find a good enough candidate for sex. He was glad that the encounter with the pimp hadn't worn him out too much and he was still horny. He could feel himself throbbing in his pants as he tried to find a good lover for his time. Suddenly, as he turned a corner, he saw a very beautiful, fair-skinned woman walking by him. Her hair was dark and her eyes were brown, her eyelashes long. She had very juicy lips and a long flowing gown, though it was ripped and tattered.

Agrippa reached out and grabbed the woman by the arm. "Excuse my intrusion, miss."

The woman looked to Agrippa with a smile. "Yes, sir, I am a prostitute. That is why such a nobly dressed gentleman like you is down here, I'm sure."

Agrippa stared back at the woman with some held back fear in his eyes. "Do you mind if I ask you for your time."

The woman gave a musing smile. "I am Genevieve. You?"

"Cornelius. Cornelius Agrippa."

"Cornelius. Pleased to meet you."

Agrippa looked at the woman in her eyes and felt like he could have known her from somewhere before. She just felt so familiar and warm to him. He didn't want to scare her with the feeling he was getting, though he felt that it was possible that she could feel the same way. "So, where can we conduct business?"

The woman nudged her head against Agrippa's shoulder as she held one of his hands with both of her own, admiring the fingers of the man as if they were golden. "I have a place."

Holding Agrippa's hand, the woman led him down a small path between some houses. Before long, they had reached a little abode among other homes. Genevieve pulled Agrippa in behind her, smiling as she looked at the man's face. Agrippa was astonished with the interior of the place. The mundane things didn't even capture his attention—a pan of bread, bowls, and a miniature kitchen inside all blurred out of focus as unusual items stood out. Inside, there were a few crystals and gems sitting on rugs in the center of the floor with a little drum that seemed of foreign origin. A huge broom sat in the front of the place as a black cat walked around and meowed freely. There was even a bunch of old manuscripts sitting on a wooden table.

Agrippa looked at the woman with astonishment. "You can read?" Somehow, he wasn't surprised by the little secretive smile placed upon Genevieve's lips. Staring back around, he captured more interesting sights—handcrafted statuettes of foreign deities, strange herb collections, and gold plates with sigils carved into them. Agrippa recognized the sigils that were carved into the plates instantly. They were symbols used to invoke planetary angels.

Agrippa looked at the woman with confusion. "You know, you need to be careful with who you bring here. You have all of these things out in the open. Don't you know that they are crucifying women such as yourself all over Europe?"

The woman laughed. "Oh, but I am safe with you."

Agrippa looked at the woman in her eyes as he hesitated, trying to play things safely before making assumptions.

"I know you," the woman said as she leaned closer towards Agrippa.

"Oh?"

"Yes. You're known quite well in secret circles, you know? I dreamed about you a long time ago."

Agrippa looked at the woman with a strange puzzled look. "Really? Dreams can be elusive, you know."

"They can also be very prophetic. You should know that very well." The woman reached over to one of her manuscripts and picked it up, handing it to Agrippa. "Look familiar?"

Agrippa grabbed the manuscript and started to thumb through it. It didn't take long for his mouth to drop in a silent gasp. "This is my book."

The woman smiled. "Yours, to an extent. You took a lot of information from a lot of sources, here and there, and made your own book. Some sort of collection of knowledge, a manual on the occult." Laughing, the woman reached her hands up to Agrippa's cheeks.

Agrippa looked at the woman with a mix of allure and distrust. "I don't like to refer to such things as the occult."

Shrugging, the woman stared at Agrippa with amusement. "Well, call it what you want to. There is only a special type of people that would study or even write about such a thing. You appeal to people such as me, people like you. We're scattered around in ignorant vacuum of a world but we are out there. I must admit, you are a very brilliant man. You look just as I dreamed of you, and the monk that copied that manuscript told me that I would find you here."

Agrippa reached his hands up to Genevieve's hands, caressing them before kissing them and looking back at her. "What do you want me to do then? Now that we have met?"

"You have an obligation to me, now."

Agrippa didn't know what to expect, though he could tell that Genevieve's eyes were expecting him to know right then and there what the woman wanted.

"Mr. Agrippa... I want you to teach me magic."

Agrippa shook his head. "With all of the many items that you have in your house? You wouldn't need me for that."

The woman shook her head. "I've collected many things in my lifetime, Mr. Agrippa. You would be surprised how much a prostitute can save in order to get secrets of the universe." Undoing the front of her dress, the woman let her breasts spill out. Her breasts were already big enough, but the areolas of her breasts were saucer sized, her nipples fat and pink. "I have studied all that I could think would be important in terms of using and understanding magic. Still, I don't know how to use it to save the life of me. Not real magic."

"Real magic?"

"Yes, real magic. Sure, I can do a love spell here and there. Make a john fall in love with me, give me his money. Clear out a small cold here and there. But a real spell? Real magic? That is all very foreign to me."

"Honestly, Genevieve, I don't think that I would be able to help you—"

"Lie all that you want, Mr. Agrippa. I know that you are a real magician." The woman rubbed her breasts against Agrippa as she licked her lips. "I've met many wise scribes, monks hiding in the church and practicing magic behind the backs of their priests. I've met witches hiding in the countryside and frauds entertaining their charming friends at parties. They are all limited in what they can do. You, however, are the real deal."

Agrippa walked up to Genevieve, as he was now standing close to her, face to face, towering over her by a few inches. Lowering his head into the woman's breasts, Agrippa started to suckle the fat nipples playfully, rubbing his hand on the woman's back. The woman purred playfully, just like a cat, as she allowed herself to come into Agrippa's arms. She was satisfied with his touch, wanting him more with each growing second. Her nipples were now perked and hard as he sucked them more, burying his face in her breasts. They were so huge, his face stuffed into them as his nose rubbed against the skin. At a moment, he reached down between the woman's legs just so that he could feel her cunt. It was wet, juicy, and tight, quite tight for a prostitute. Even his wife wasn't this well maintained, even before having children.

Dropping his pants, Agrippa grabbed his hardened cock out of her underwear and rubbed the head against the woman's leg. She pulled back instantly, teasing the man as she giggled.

Agrippa sighed, shaking his head. "I don't think you understand about the risks involved with teaching you magic, woman. The things that I do outside of the sights of man are no business for anyone to learn. It's dangerous."

"You don't think that I am constantly living a life of danger already?" Genevieve dropped her entire dress now. She was completely naked. "I am not afraid. If anyone here is afraid, it's only you. You have no need to fear. I am a grown woman and I can handle myself." Genevieve reached down and started to feel her busy, fingering herself deeply.

Agrippa gulped. "Well. I can tell by your energy and eyes that you have a high inclination for magic."

The woman nodded. "I do. I just need a good teacher. A friend of mine did a natal chart for me on a scroll. Perhaps you can take a look at it after we're done."

Nodding, Agrippa stepped towards the woman and started to feel on her nipples again. "That I can."

Genevieve giggled. "You better not just fuck me, pay me, and run out." Kneeling on the ground, Genevieve stuck her ass out as she continued to finger her cunt. "Now, please fuck me from behind. I'm not trying to get pregnant."

That was the moment that their first ritual started. Sex was magic in itself. Agrippa firmly believes that, and he could tell by the working of the woman's ass muscles that she believes in it, too. His cock had to wrestle to get into her asshole and her backside was nice and soft. He grabbed it and held onto it as he worked his cock in, deeper and deeper. The woman held her hands against the rug, seeming to take the new fucking like a soldier. She made a few soft moaning sounds at first, as if she was trying to avoid being too loud or animalistic. The black cat ran out of the house as the two humans went at it, fucking each other roughly. Agrippa beat into Genevieve's ass as he watched her hair pour down over her back, inspiring him to pull it a bit.

"Ouch!" Genevieve said for a moment before moaning and purring again.

She likes it, Agrippa realized as he pulled the woman's hair and fucked her forcibly in the ass. He felt like he was fitting pretty well into her, as tight as she was, and she was gripping his cock pretty tight. At times, he would spank her to get her moving a little faster in order to keep up with his rhythms, and she was retracting to make the friction more intense. Agrippa really hoped that she would let him come inside of her when he was done since so many prostitutes were afraid of cum. Agrippa had to admit that Genevieve seemed a little more educated and relaxed than the average prostitute, so he doubted that she would have any irritating requests.

The more that he fucked her, the more Agrippa felt something stirring inside of him. The action of fucking wasn't just an action that felt meaningless. Usually, when Agrippa made theses tours into slums and prostitute areas, the man felt like he was only looking for a quick fuck. He wasn't looking for any connection or even affection for that matter. Even so, with each pumping of the dick and pull of the hair, Agrippa felt love. For each purring sound egging him on to the differentiating highs and lows of moaning flowing from Genevieve's mouth with occasional screams, he could feel a love developing. The whole feeling was spreading and his heart was open. He was even convinced that she felt the same way, also.

"Oh God, don't stop!" Genevieve's huge breasts swung back and forth under her as Agrippa fucked her, whining and moaning exiting her lips. "You've got a huge cock. Goddamn, Mr. Agrippa!" The woman gritted her teeth as she felt the cock being forced into her more, trying to take it with little complaint. Even her hand, which had been obediently fingering her cunt as she was getting ass fucked, had to get a better grip on the ground. The friction of the ass fucking had been getting more intense. She buried her head to the ground, trying to take it the best that she could.

Up until that point, Agrippa was convinced that he had never had a fuck session as good as the one he was having now. For one, his wife would have never let him fuck him in the ass, let along for strictly pleasurable reasons. They only had sex to ensure that the children had been born. He loved his wife tenderly, like the other extension of his soul. This woman, however, was something special as well. Even before she had made him feel this good, she had connected with him instantly. She had shown an interest in magic, something that he was never used to seeing exemplified in a woman before. It was almost like a dream that he was afraid to wake up from. Would she continue to be this interested, once he showed her the secrets he had to share?

The woman was screaming now, her ass sore from the fucking as her pussy juices just poured down her legs. Agrippa would reach down and lick it up from time to time, getting a good taste of her. She was sweet, as if she ate lots of fruit. From time to time, he could reach up far enough to grab some of her tits as they flopped back and forth so ridiculously. Those breasts were huge and Agrippa thought that the woman was blessed to have them.

Agrippa groaned loudly as he felt his cum

shoot inside of the woman. He could feel it leaving him, hot and sticky, as the woman's motions moved obediently with his, stopping as he stopped as well.

Agrippa pulled up from behind her, looking down at her with fiery eyes. "How much do I owe you?" he said as he was sweating profusely.

"Free of monetary charge," Genevieve responded.

Agrippa continued to breathe heavily, trying to catch his breath.

"Teach me magic," the woman ordered as she turned around, staring Agrippa dead in the face.

The magician nodded. "Okay. I can teach you magic. That will be my payment for sex."

"And future sex sessions."

Agrippa wiped some sweat from his brow. "Okay, that's fair enough. Where should we practice the magic? Here?"

The woman was sweating heavily as well, seeming to have enjoyed the sex as she moved towards Agrippa. "Wherever you would like." She pressed her chest against the man, hugging him tight. Her embrace was warm and comfortable to Agrippa. Before long, they were laying down with each other, snuggling and enjoying a lazy evening together. Agrippa could see his family the next day.

There were more sex sessions to come.

Usually, the two would meet in the slums and fuck each other's brains out. Genevieve would eventually warm up to Agrippa fucking her in her pussy as long as he pulled out as promised. The woman never did get pregnant, which was good. In many scenarios, she would sit on top of him, dominating the situation. That was something Agrippa liked about her, unlike his wife that had always expected him to do all of the work.

During the weekends, especially on Sundays, when they had a chance to be with each other, Agrippa would come to the woman's house and teach her magic. If they were lucky, Agrippa would find some storage space in a nearby school. The woman learned quickly. Before long, she was practicing divination with much skill, able to pick up information through geomancy and astrology at an alarming rate. Agrippa looked through the woman's natal chart, something that had been on the secret lovers' to do list for a while. He understood her nature now quite clearly and why they meshed so well together. It was as if they were twins sent from heaven to find each other on Earth.

"You are truly an extraordinary woman," Agrippa told her once. "I've never met another woman that could entertain these subjects, let alone believe in this stuff."

The woman laughed. "I come from a long line of gypsies, my friend. Personally, my family found a way to assimilate in France and even Germany has been a good home to me. Still, I cannot help but feel more comfortable living by myself, studying the magic arts."

"Yet you feel that you have never practiced them?"

"As I said, I can do small things. But I've never been able to do magic. Real magic."

Agrippa smiled. "You will by the time this spring is up."

The magician had been correct. Genevieve did her first major magic spell, nearly a few months later, with what seemed to be little effort. The couple had taken some herbs, boiling water, and a pot. With some incantations, Genevieve stood over the pot and worked her hands over it in a circular motion. It took a total of ten minutes, but before long, Genevieve had breathed in the scent from the water and become completely invisible.

Coming back into view for Agrippa, the woman grinned, beaming from ear to ear. "I did it!"

Agrippa could only smile back, proud of how quickly his pupil had been learning magic.

Over the next couple of months, Genevieve would produce more tricks and spells. She had a grandmother in the country that had been suffering from a severe illness. After creating a tonic with Agrippa's guidance, she had been able to completely heal the ailing woman in a way that every other doctor had failed to do. The invisibility spell came in handy for Genevieve when she was traveling at night as well, keeping her safe from bandits and men that would have bad intentions for her. In a short amount of time, she had learned levitation, teleportation, and even gained a strong second sight for revealing prophecies. She was surprised with how much she could do.

Agrippa had come to visit Genevieve one day, yet she was nowhere to be found. After waiting in her place for a while after realizing the door was open, he eventually decided it was time to go home.

He heard a meow at his feet. Looking down, he saw the black cat.

"You!" he said with a smile. "We had thought you had run off on us."

Suddenly, the cat started to twitch wildly. It slowly became amorphous as it transformed, a shadowy figure forming from it that shot up in a human shape and became more corporeal.

Agrippa looked in shock. "Genevieve?"

The woman formed out of the shadow, her skin full and naked, her face smiling vibrantly as she was back to her old self. "Yes, dear. It's me."

Agrippa shook his head. "Where did you learn this trick?"

Genevieve looked at Agrippa's face, shocked that it was looked so worried and concerned. "Well, from your private notes, of course." The woman pointed at her wooden table where a ripped out piece of paper sat. "One of those pages from that secret book you keep."

Agrippa stood up and grabbed the woman by the arms, looking at her with furious eyes. "Don't you ever do that trick again. Never again!"

The woman shook her head. "What's the matter? I don't understand?"

"Never again!"

Genevieve grew angry. "Get the fuck off of me!" She shook out of Agrippa's grip. As the man reached into to grab her again, the woman started to slap him in the face repeatedly.

The magician backed up, looking at the woman like she was crazy.

"Get out of here!" she said as she pointed at the door. "You crazy buffoon! I never want to see you again!"

Agrippa looked at the woman with sorrowful eyes. "You don't mean that."

"Yes, I do mean that. You think you can treat me any way just because you taught me some tricks? What's the matter? You don't like a woman learning the secret things that you have learned?"

Agrippa shook his head. "No, it's not that at all. The magic you performed is part of the dark arts. If it's done incorrectly, bad things can happen. You must—"

"I must nothing. Fuck you! Get out of here!"

Looking at the woman with sadness, Agrippa shook his head as he finally gave in. "Okay. You've got it. I'll leave."

"If I ever see you here again, I will kill you!"

The magician walked out calmly, not even looking behind him as the naked woman started to cry.

Months passed before the magician would even hear of the woman or see her again, though he thought about her daily. Agrippa had tried everything he could to get his mind off the woman, even taking a break from his magic and spending more time with his family. It was of no use.

Agrippa thought of getting out of Cologne. When he would do it, however, he was not sure. He had had enough of the city. Having been born there, he knew that he was a traveling man. There were no wishes to live and die in the same place that he had wanted to escape since his youth. If he left, however, he wanted to make sure he could bring his family with him.

As he walked through the streets one day, looking for some work to take his time as he was on leave from the military, Agrippa could hear a crowd gathering. Curious, he rushed to where he saw a mob of people shouting and carrying pitchforks and raising fists. Most of them were screaming at the top of their lungs, almost seeming to be in an angered state of frenzy. As he approached, however, things became clearer.

"Burn the witches!" Agrippa could hear the people saying in different tones and voices, chanting together.

The mob had spread to the sides of the street to let a large group of people pass through. Agrippa looked in the middle of the crowd to see some magistrates, judges, and executioners marching along a variety of people in chains. Agrippa noticed that one of the chained individuals was a man but most of them were women. Before long, he felt his heart freeze as he saw Genevieve in rags among the chained prisoners, marching along with fear in her eyes.

"Burn the witches!" the crowd chanted. "Burn the witches! Burn the witches!"

Agrippa's mouth dropped as he thought frantically on what he could do.

"Let the woman go."

Agrippa stood in the office of one of the principle magistrates working on Genevieve's case. He had done quite a lot of work to find out exactly where he needed to go and who he needed to talk to in order to free Genevieve. Hoping that the man would have a sense of dignity, Agrippa would do his best to clear any misunderstandings.

The magistrate looked at Agrippa with a laugh. "Let her go? But she is a witch."

Agrippa shook his head. "She is not a witch. Doesn't she have anyone to defend her?"

"Who would defend a witch?"

"I told you. She is not a witch. Where are you keeping her now?"

"She is being handled with our guards,

until she confesses."

Agrippa grabbed his hair as he shouted at the ceiling. "This is inhumane!"

"God is not inhumane, Mr. Agrippa." The magistrate got comfortable in his chair as he stared up at the frantic Agrippa. "Many people testified that they saw this woman turning into all types of animals—black cats, hogs, dogs, snakes, and even lizards. These are animals of the devil, and Genevieve is a wife of the devil."

Agrippa shook his head. "Come on, magistrate. This doesn't make any sense. You are speaking of things that happen in fairy tales."

The magistrate's face flushed as he looked at Agrippa with anger. "Do you believe that our Lord teaches us fairy tales?"

Agrippa looked at the magistrate with angered eyes. "No."

The magistrate grinned. "Our Lord teaches us about the dark forces that exist in our world. You think that he made all of those things up? You are a fool to believe such nonsense."

Agrippa pressed his hands on his hips as he took a deep breath. "I will defend this woman."

The man looked at Agrippa with wide eyes of disbelief. "You must be kidding."

"I've defended witches before in other courts of law. I can do this now."

The magistrate nodded. "I see. Well, everyone has a chance to prove their innocence in being a witch. I guess it wouldn't hurt for her to have you by her side."

"Thank you."

"I will see you in court then?"

Agrippa walked out.

Agrippa did all that he could for the woman. He went to the courthouse and fought for her. As she stood in the room, chained like an animal and covered with bruises from harsh beatings, he told the court as much evidence he had that they were wrong. Working hard to prove that Genevieve was not a witch, he brought in items from her home, questioned judges intensively, and even spoke on Genevieve's behalf. In the end, it didn't work out and Agrippa failed. Genevieve would be executed at the stake.

The magician couldn't bring himself to come to the execution. He only shook his head for teaching the woman magic in the first place. He had told her before how dangerous the arts were, how much they could get someone in trouble. Even if she didn't heed his warnings, he could only blame himself for being pulled so easily into the charms of another woman.

Genevieve had been blessed—for that much, the man could be sure. In another lifetime, as a man, she could have been a great scholar, well liked for her wisdom though a bit eccentric, feared for her strange grasp of things beyond human knowledge.

Agrippa wished, at times, that they could have switched roles, and the woman could have still been alive instead, saved from the hells of their persecuting times.

Now, in a university well away from Cologne, Agrippa collected his notes. He suffered in silence with memories of the past and thoughts of the present. He knew that, even in his hard work to the military, academia, and other fields of work, he would always be an outsider. Very few people had ever come close to understanding him, let alone allow him to feel normal. With Genevieve long gone, all he could do was remember a time when magic really meant something beyond the uncanny. The time that magic brought him as powerful and pleasurable as love was the most extraordinary time in his life.

7 BONE ME ALREADY

For a comedy bar, the place was really quiet. That was the first thing that any comedian noticed when they came into Sal's Comedy Joint. The patrons were very rough looking and didn't seem to be very nice. Truckers, construction men, and shady characters in business suits seemed to make up the clientele. The strong smell of alcohol, cigarettes, and sweat filled the place like a disgusting sauna. Perhaps this was where all the lowlifes of the world came for a good laugh?

Kelsey didn't really like the place. She tried not to stereotype people or put down the patrons in her head, which was pretty hard for a comedian not to do. A part of her wondered if it would ease the tension by just letting loose and allowing the patrons to amuse her. Maybe she could even think of a way to include them in her jokes for the night. No, she thought, don't worry about all that. Just focus on the show. Make it good.

Recommended to the place by another female comedian, Kelsey hoped that the place would be good. She had been to a lot of dumps. She had talked to the owner a bit and he had seemed nice at least. Kelsey just hoped the place would warm up to her senses eventually. As Kelsey took a look at all the other comedians that had showed up for the show, she noticed that it was still kind of early, about 9 o'clock. She was a little relieved to see that all of the standup talent tonight would be women. At the same time, she couldn't help but also feel a little weird about that obvious fact. Each of the ladies looked pretty in their own right: some of them dressed in business suits, some casual, and others looking like full on whores. There were comedians in nothing but lingerie and pouf hair as if they stepped out of a dirty 80s magazine. The customer base of the bar seemed to be an all-male crowd. Were any of them really ready for this? Kelsey wondered if they wanted to be objectified for a laugh. Perhaps she'd see some raunchy burlesque-type humor.

Looking to the door of the place, Kelsey was happy to finally see the organizer for the event show up. In an earlier meeting, he had told Kelsey that he owned the place. He was an older, middle-aged man, bald at the top with the sides of his head holding on to the last pieces of ruffled orange hair. Being a tall guy, his tacky jacket and worn-out pants with patches looked more like a bum's wear than that of the organizer of an event or the owner of a bar. Kelsey had to laugh. On looks alone, the guy could have been a great standup comedian or at least a circus clown. In a profession like that, he wouldn't even need makeup.

"Fucking ass hasn't paid me yet," one of the girls said under her breath. "Cheapskate."

Kelsey looked at the woman inquisitively. "I thought we get paid after the show?"

The woman looked at Kelsey with a very dismissive look. "Um, maybe you're supposed to get paid after the show. I'm the headliner. I require a payment before the show and a payment after the show."

"Oh." Kelsey just let the woman look at her wildly. There was no need to engage her in any argument or battle of wits. That would have been a waste of her time and energy she would need for her act.

"Have you ever done comedy here before?" The headlining woman looked Kelsey up and down. "I don't think that I've ever seen you here before."

"Nope," Kelsey said. "First time here."

"Wow." The woman smiled. "You're in for a treat. That's really all I have to say."

Kelsey looked at the woman with a smile as she extended her hand for a shake. "What's your name?"

The woman walked away.

"Fine then," Kelsey said before strolling over to the bar.

There was a bartender wiping down one of the glasses. He had just finished serving a big burly man that smelled like a pack of cigarettes.

"You got any wine here?" Kelsey asked politely.

The bartender looked up from his glass. He chuckled as he stared at the female comedian in the eyes with a condescending glare. "Wine? What do you think this is, the Taj Mahal?"

The smelly tobacco man stifled a harsh chuckle from his closed lips, staring down at his drink.

"Fine," Kelsey said, rolling her eyes as she placed a hand on her hip. "Give me your best beer, I guess. How much?"

The bartender grinned as he looked down, shuffling through a bunch of drinks in a nearby cooler. He seemed to have found something good, pulling out a beer bottle from a cluttered row of different brands. "You're a performer, baby. It's on the house."

Kelsey took an open beer bottle from the bartender as she sneered, "Don't call me 'baby.'" Kelsey knocked her head back to take a swig. Before her third gulp, her head was lifting up again. She pulled the bottle away, wiping her mouth with a disgusted look on her face. "Yuck! This tastes like piss!"

The bartender laughed. "If you can't stand our drinks, lady, maybe you need to book more comedy shows at the Holiday Inn."

Kelsey eyed the bartender with a sharp look. "You're really funny. You should be your own comedian."

"No thanks. That's a woman's job."

Kelsey had to step away from the bar. The nerve of that man, she thought. She was completely disgusted with his rude comments and foul behavior. Having his little man buddy there to laugh at his completely not funny jokes angered her as well. Maybe I ought to have my revenge, Kelsey thought. The bar was full of chauvinist yokels, it seemed. Perhaps she needed to show them a thing or two once she got on stage. Perhaps—

Kelsey's train of thought stopped like a wreck as she bumped into the venue owner. There he was. The clown, Kelsey thought insultingly. Kelsey had almost forgotten that she needed to talk to him, and now, she was even more flustered than when she first entered the place.

The owner smiled. "Kelsey! I'm glad you were able to make it."

Kelsey put her beer on the nearest table as she looked up at the owner. "Um listen... John, right? We need to talk."

John's brows lifted in a puzzled expression. "Is something wrong?"

Kelsey grabbed John by the arm and pulled him over to the side of the table with her beer waiting patiently. "Yes, John. There's a lot wrong with this. I'm very pissed with what's going on right now. You've got truck punks and bad breath hillbillies running around with no manners. There are women walking around half-naked as if I'm on the set of a porno. I feel like you didn't really tell me what I was getting myself into here. What the hell is going on?"

John lowered his head a bit. "I'm sorry to see you uncomfortable here."

"Hell yeah, I'm uncomfortable!" Kelsey frowned. "This is like some demon cesspool or something? I just got to know: am I here for comedy?"

"I only work to offer the best comedy in town," John said. "Look, I understand if this seems already like a bit much for you, but I would hope that you could wait things out-"

"Gentlemen and gentlemen!"

The loud, booming voice came from an announcer on the stage. Kelsey and John looked towards the stage immediately with all the other patrons of the bar, their eyes transfixed on the MC for the show. A huge spotlight from overhead captured the beauty perfectly. She was a tall, leggy brunette wearing fishnet stockings and a top hat. Her torso was decorated in nothing but a set of bra and panties that matched her lipstick. Her lips were decorated in a ruby tone as she smiled, a black mole teasing her left cheek. "I'm Chelsea, your hostess for the evening! I know you've been missing me this whole week. So, let mama know... are you big boys ready to laugh?"

The men started hollering and hooting, banging their fists on the table as they looked up at the woman with excitement.

Chelsea was pouting playfully, trailing a hand down the middle of her torso. "That was kind of weak." She sighed. "I said, are you ready to laugh?"

Guys were whistling throughout the bar as Kelsey looked up at the stage, holding back some rage as her fists shook. What kind of a comedy hostess was this freak? What kind of a crowd was she catering to? Kelsey thought that she was going to be sick.

Chelsea shook her head. "You know what, guys? I don't think you're ready to laugh up here." Chelsea pointed at her smile playfully. "Oh no. I think you're ready to laugh... down there." Pointing towards a man's crotch as he watched gleefully from the audience, the crowd got even more rowdy. Drinks slammed on tables as whistles still continued, men begging for more.

Kelsey couldn't believe this. Was this hostess real?

"Oh yeah. That's what I like to hear. That makes me want to tell some... jokes." Chelsea threw her top hat into the crowd. A lucky guy stood up from where he was sitting and caught it.

Trying to think of ways to calm down and be patient, Kelsey could feel her heart racing. This couldn't be a normal comedy show. She had walked into a horny dog fest! It was moments like this that she wished she could have had a manager.

"Okay, guys," Chelsea said as she started to strut on stage, holding the microphone firmly in her hands. "You know, being a hostess is hard work sometimes. I was always told that I had to feed my guests. A lady tries to be neat, but you wouldn't believe it—I always end up giving out sloppy seconds!"

Men laughed throughout the seedy establishment, clapping their hands and hollering.

"Oh yeah," Chelsea said in a breathy voice. "That gets my oven hot. Keep laughing boys." Chelsea reached up and undid her bra. Grabbing it in her hands, she threw it into the face of a happy horn dog patron.

"This is ridiculous," Kelsey said as her eyes widened.

The owner looked down at Kelsey with a laugh.

Kelsey looked back at John with anger. "You're damned if you think I'm doing shit like this."

Chelsea was now slowly pacing back and forth on stage, massaging her nipples with one hand and holding the microphone with another. "You know, scrubbing out my oven before company comes over is pretty rough too," Chelsea said, "and soooo lonely, honestly." She pulled down her panties as the men's eyes were fixed on her. "Really, it is. Let me show you."

The whistles filled the bar once again. Raised fists and loud shouts filled the air. Kelsey couldn't believe this. She thought that things would get wild, but this was beyond wild. Such a stage performance like this was an insult to human civilization everywhere, she thought to herself. She was way too smart for all of this. Her limit had been reached minutes ago. Earlier, she had been fighting thoughts of walking out, and she still thought of it. She could even have made a big scene and cursed everyone out there—the horny male customers and the degrading female comedians. A middle finger could have been raised as she called them idiotic and worthless to society. If she stormed out, she was pretty sure she could get John to chase after her, plead for her to come back, and do the show. Then she would flick him off personally, tell him what a chauvinist pig he was, and get the next cab she could. That would make her a strong and defiant memory for this horrid establishment to remember her as a comedian with morals, one to not put up with such a degrading show.

Still, she couldn't look away. Even in her anger and her want to be angry, she couldn't get out of this show. Not just yet.

Even when the hostess sat on the stage and spread her legs, Kelsey could not walk away. She just stared blankly as Chelsea had started to shove her hand into her cunt. The fingers went in pretty quickly without any big preparation, and Kelsey immediately thought of what a slut the hostess must have been. In a few pressings, she had already jammed half of her hand inside of her cunt. Chelsea's moaning filled the bar, her head leaning back as her hair brushed against the stage. Her ass muscles seemed to squeeze with each pushing of her hands and fingers into her pussy.

There was a part of Kelsey that hated everything about what she was seeing before her. She hated that the hostess had a name that was closely similar to hers in sound. She hated how this hostess seemed to derive pleasure from a horn dog audience at what seemed like supposedly a comedy show. She hated how all of these guys were just whores for entertainment. The entire scene pissed Kelsey off completely. But there was something that Kelsey liked about it, and she could feel that she liked it immensely. She could even see the sexual thrill of the hostess on stage and for a minute, Kelsey was a little envious. Even as a comedian who had killed shows with success, Kelsey had never received applause like this. The hostess, in some weird and perverted way, was loved by her audience. That embarrassed Kelsey even more. As Chelsea moved her hand to feel deep inside of her own cunt, starting to moan for the appeasement of the men's appetite, Kelsey could only watch and get lost in the action as well.

"Ohhh yeah...," Kelsey said as she drove her hand in deep, even her wrists slipping in at points. Damn, her pussy was big, and her hands didn't seem smaller than average. "Got some bread crust."

The guys laughed as the woman continued to dig her cunt out, clapping loudly and watching with unyielding attention.

"There's some... hmmm, stuff from the cake." Kelsey was moaning constantly with each forced hand movement.

Kelsey felt herself getting hot and

bothered. She also noticed that she was getting a bit wet as well. God, what was happening to her?

Suddenly, the woman started to moan really loud, her eyes widening as she faked an orgasm. At least I can tell she's faking it, Kelsey thought. It seemed highly obvious to her, though it really excited the men to a high level.

The hostess lifted up her hand and suckled on the juice that ran down her hand. "Mmmm... leftovers."

Hooting and hollering, the men seemed like animals that couldn't be contained in their seats. The scene was like something out of the old West. Some men threw their trucker hats in midair or towards the stage, others just shouting in elation.

"You like that, don't you?" Chelsea said as she started to stand up. "I'm sure some of the leftovers I tasted were from some of you."

Kelsey rolled her eyes. Oh brother, she thought, save the horrible ass kissing.

"Wow, guys... you really know how to get a girl worked up. But I'm just the hostess. I'm here for quickies." Chelsea grinned. "Your first real performers for the night, however, should be a two-course meal for all of you."

Many men were already clapping.

"Oh, you know who they are already," Chelsea said deviously. "They're two of your favorite ladies. The funny, the quirky, the sexy... midnight girls!" Chelsea started clapping as she ran off stage, urging the audience on as they followed in a warm welcome.

The first comedians came on stage. One was a cute, bubbly Asian woman wearing some shiny green lingerie with dollar bills stuffed in them. The other woman was a blonde, wearing a gray business suit with a hat to match. Both had slender builds, the blonde slightly taller than her friend.

"Um, Roxy?" the blonde said to her Asian friend with a faux look of confusion. "Why do you have money stuffed up in your private regions?"

"Because, Foxy," Roxy said back to her buxom business partner, "I heard that sex sells."

Many of the customers were laughing already.

Foxy raised her blonde eyebrows with interest. "Oh? And so, if sex sells, what does that have to do with putting money in your lingerie?"

Roxy shrugged. "Well, I figured if I got to sell this stuff I've got, I better have some change."

More laughs came.

"Really? How do you figure that you'd need change?"

"Well... some guys come up short."

The place was a riot. Kelsey looked around for a moment to see the many guys laughing. Really? These jokes were supposed to be funny? If this was funny, then why the hell was she not laughing? The only thing that Kelsey could figure out of the whole thing was that the guys liked laughing at the women as they sexually humiliated themselves. To Kelsey, it was a bit sadist.

Foxy had to wait until the laughter died in order to make sure the rest of the skit would be audible. "Roxy, I'm sorry, but this isn't really making that much sense. Saying that sex sells and you need extra cash for change and everything."

Roxy seemed to be insulted. "Well, how doesn't it make sense?" Roxy looked Foxy up and down. "I mean, you're a working girl, aren't you?"

Foxy's eyes widened. "Well, um, yes, I am."

"Oh? And what kind of work is it that you do anyway?"

Foxy's eyes looked back and forth. "Well, I'm a consultant?"

"I guess that could be interesting. Who consults you?"

"Guys at Sal's Comedy Joint."

The place was filled with laughs once again. This isn't funny, damn it, Kelsey thought.

Roxy looked surprised, staring out at the audience before looking back at Foxy. "Really, you do? Well, that's funny. I do a lot of work for the guys at that very place, too!"

"Really? What is it that you do anyway?"

"I'm a cash drawer."

"... Do you mean a cashier?"

"No, I'm literally a cash drawer. Guys

open me and fuck me. There's no mystery there, girlfriend."

The horn dogs were laughing all over the place. Kelsey giggled a bit. Damn, she thought to herself. That must have been an accident. Maybe she was just laughing at the fact that the woman was a total slut.

"Really?" Foxy asked. "Gee, that's kind of hot." She traced a hand on one of Roxy's breasts. Some men whistled; others egged them on verbally. "You mind to show me how a transaction would work?"

Roxy nodded as she rubbed a hand on Foxy's waist. "Well, okay. But first, you got to get me out of these stupid clothes and money. And you got to take off that suit. If we don't do that, this won't work very well."

"Okay." Foxy pulled down Roxy's bottom piece quickly, letting it slide to the woman's thighs as cash flew everywhere. "Like this?"

The men watched in what seemed to be the closest to silence since the show began.

"Yeah," Roxy said as she pulled off the bottom piece completely, throwing it into the audience as she looked her friend eye to eye. "Don't forget to take off the bra. The guys like to see everything, you know."

Everyone's eyes were focused on the stage.

"Sure, that makes sense," Foxy said as she reached over for her friend's bra and completely took it off, throwing it into the audience.

Roxy spun around slowly to showcase her figure to the audience. Even Kelsey had to admit that Roxy was a very sexually appealing woman. She was hot.

Roxy pointed at Foxy. "Okay, now you have to do it. It's your turn."

Foxy looked a bit insulted as she pressed a hand against her chest. "My turn? You must be kidding! I am a respectable woman."

"No one's going to respect you if you can't follow up on seeing what you asked to see in the first place."

Foxy scratched her head. "What did I ask to see?"

"A transaction. And you have to be completely naked to see one of those."

Foxy shrugged. "Okay, I guess that makes sense."

Helping her friend take off her business clothes, Roxy grinned as she could see Foxy's black lingerie draped over her pale and rosy body. Patrons cheered for Foxy as she pulled off her own bra and panties seductively, winking at the audience as she finally did it.

"You look really good, Foxy," Roxy said before taking the blonde to the ground. That was the last thing either of them would say for the rest of the night.

The crowd watched in excitement, urging the two lovers on as they started to eat each other out in a 69 position. Roxy was gripping onto Foxy's ass as she stuffed her face into her lap, licking away wildly. Foxy handled her friend just the same, their faces buried deep as they licked and slurped inside of each other, moaning on occasion. The guys laughed as they could even see the women reaching into each other's ass cracks, fingering each other teasingly.

God, Kelsey thought to herself. These girls were real freaks. These guys were maniacs. Kelsey felt so weird as she watched the whole thing, seeing the guys acting so frenzied like that. A moan escaped Kelsey's lips. As her hands reached up to her face in instant fear and embarrassment, Kelsey looked to her side to see John smirking at her, amused.

Oh no, Kelsey thought to herself, please don't let this freak think I approve this. Kelsey looked at John with horror as she saw she suddenly found his creepy and homely looks favorable. This show was bringing out something weird in her.

The girls continued to have a chow-down on stage. Their bodies pressed against each other as if they were wrestling erotically. They rolled a few times, remaining safe and never going over the edge of the stage. At times, they would pull their heads up to gasp for air, only to press down again and continuing eating. For some other moments, one of the ladies only pressed down further, grabbing the ass cheeks tight as if they were afraid that they would lose each other in the process of pussy eating.

Kelsey looked over to the sides of the bar. Some of the female comedians were still out there, waiting on the sidelines instead of backstage. Their faces were all very turned on and sensual, panting, with eyelashes battering. God, even the women were getting into this! A few of the ladies were even fingering themselves. This erotic show had effects on others other than just the men? Kelsey had felt like a sideshow attraction that had just realized her predicament, running into other oddities like her. Never did she think that she could find something pleasurable in a show like this. If anything, she wished she could run. Now, she felt way in too deep. She liked this all too much.

The two women climaxed on stage. Kelsey could feel it this time. She knew it was real. It was as if she were having an awakening. She thought back to when the hostess climaxed earlier, realizing that that had been real as well. Wow—the entire time, Kelsey thought that these women were just throwing on a show for some slaver-like males looking to get their jollies off. Now, she realized that this was for more than just the men. She could feel a connection with every comedian in the room, and the audience was being brought to life by them all.

Roxy and Foxy got up, leaving the stage in a soaked mess. The hostess got back up and guided the show as nicely as she had been doing before. Act after act came up. Kelsey saw a lot of funny women, spewing out jokes with sexual innuendos and some outright raunchy lines as well. It always seemed like the jokes would last for possibly two minutes and a sexual act or rendezvous would fill ten to twenty. Kelsey was surprised with what could fill three hours. She had probably seen thirteen or fourteen girls go up so far, and there were still ten left.

"And now, gentlemen and gentlemen," the hostess said with a teasing smile. "We've reached the halfway point of our show. It's time to pull up the headliner for the evening, Lilith the firecracker!"

The crowd exploded with cheering and clapping. As hyped-up and wild as the crowd had been the entire night, Kelsey was sure that this was the most excited they had been.

The first woman from earlier in the night stepped on stage and Kelsey immediately felt anger towards her. Bitch, she thought to herself.

"Hey guys," Lilith started as she seemed to showcase her breasts, undoing her top. "I've been fucking men for millennium after millennium, and I've got to tell you: my pussy sure is tired."

The crowd was in a huge uproar as Lilith strutted back and forth on stage, shaking her ass.

"You know," Lilith said, "taking over human bars and using them as places to take over the minds of gullible human beings and make demonic babies can sure be fun. At the same time, it's a lot of work and is not always funny."

The men were laughing again. Though she failed to find the joke, Kelsey was laughing too.

"Now, I have a new person to break in tonight, as I do once every week." Lilith looked straight at Kelsey. "Kelsey, you'll be my volunteer."

Kelsey looked to both of her sides to make sure it wasn't her that Lilith was calling. Still, she knew that Lilith was calling her, and it made Kelsey very nervous. "Me?" she said, looking back at the redhead beauty.

"Yes, dear," the woman said. "My powers cannot be denied."

Kelsey slowly walked up to the stage. She stood and stared into Lilith's eyes.

"Now, Kelsey," Lilith began, "do you know what I am?"

Kelsey shook her head.

Lilith took her hand and rubbed Kelsey's forehead. "The Sumerians knew me. The Hebrews knew me. Many people of the desert feared my name." The woman smiled. "I am Lilith."

"Lilith."

"Men that feared me told horrific stories about me. They made me into a monster. My power was subdued, suppressed, talked about like some witch of a fairy tale. Some would say that I am the original witch. Do not fear me."

"I won't."

Lilith nodded. "You will be one of mine, like the many women and men in this room. You shall have sex with the men here. We will produce many offspring for my cause. It is what we do as night women, as succubae. But first, in order to take on your new fate, you must have sex with me."

Kelsey nodded. "Of course."

Lilith pulled Kelsey close. "Now, let's make them laugh."

The women disrobed quickly to their audience's approval. Kelsey's body was exposed on stage, sweating from the heat radiating in Lilith's eyes. The comedian could tell that the succubus was powerful and she wouldn't dare defy her. Kelsey let the woman trail her hand down her skin, rub her ass, and suckle her breasts as she pulled her in. Kelsey moaned. A few fingers found their way in Kelsey's cunt and the woman moaned again.

"Let me treat you now," Lilith said was a smile.

Kelsey forgot that an audience was watching her at the moment. She forgot that a crowd of men and women was getting their jollies off from seeing the two women on stage, fondling each other. Lilith got on top of Kelsey and, immediately, Kelsey could tell that Lilith always got on top. Lilith's fingers continued to handle Kelsey for a while, which was fun in itself. Even so, those fingers would soon be replaced with Lilith's mouth, licking at Kelsey's pussy with a furious hurricane tongue.

Kelsey twitched and moaned as she moved back and forth, feeling the demoness dive into her. Her mind was becoming blank. She didn't think about walking into the bar, or realizing the bar was a sex pit, or even that it was the house and cover of a strange supernatural entity beyond her human understanding. All she knew was that right now, a tongue was pleasuring her better than any male cock she had ever felt penetrate her at any time. She had fucked a lot of comedians, stage managers, and even audience members from time to time in her life away from the stage, but nothing compared to Lilith. Kelsey couldn't have even thought about what a hypocrite she had been to judge the entire bar for its sexual mannerisms. The comedian was completely under their control.

Kelsey opened her eyes in a moment of deep sexual arousal and penetration when she realized that no one was on top of her. She was still on stage, still feeling her cunt getting lickcd deeply, and even her nipples felt like they were being toyed with. Lilith, however, now flew over her, not laying a physical hand on her. With the mere glowing of her eyes, Lilith was handling Kelsey's body with some invisible extension of her energy, going deep inside of the woman and making her one of hers. As Kelsey felt herself getting fucked so hard and deep, yet so sensually, it wasn't long before she had an orgasm.

With the headliner finishing her act, Kelsey's new life had begun.

"You're up," Lilith said as she stepped off the stage, giving it to Kelsey.

�☙

A comedy show was ending at a small open mic in a coffee shop. As the attendees exited the door, Rebecca sighed and zipped up her backpack filled with notepads of material.

"You were pretty funny tonight," someone told her from behind.

Rebecca turned around to see a beautiful lady wearing shades, smiling.

"Thanks," Rebecca said as she returned a smile to the woman.

"This place is a bit of a dump," the woman said. "You should talk to the owner of the bar I perform at. You would be perfect to get a gig there. I'm Kelsey, by the way."

8 MOB BROADS

There was some soft muttering near the altar. Someone was praying in the Big City Catholic Church, trying to cleanse her heart of all the sins she could remember. The praying visitor was a woman, an old wrinkled lady with her gray hair covered in a bonnet. Her dress was very worn and tacky looking. Her temperament would seem sweet to one that didn't know her history. As she prayed, it was hard to keep track with what she was saying. Words came hard for the woman in her old age, and she kept stumbling over her words. She was just an old woman visiting from out of town, trying to put a dark past behind her. Still, as she looked at her gloved hands and tried to see past the invisible blood that seemed to never go away, she didn't know if she would ever transcend it all. The darkness seemed to be an eternal part of her life.

As she tried to go through the final names that she could remember from her mob days—Sal, Big Joe, Crazy Lou, Hank, other bosses, and enforcers—she realized that their faces never really went away. She had left the Big City a long time ago with the dreams of living a quiet life and letting go of a rebellious spirit. The mob girl that she had grown to be was thrown to the side, days of working as a bartender spit on and cursed. At night, she would be surprised to find her heart beating, banging against her chest as if it were banging on the door and bringing back the only face she had really known in an exclusively loving way.

"Sal," she whispered under her breath, kneeled down on the ground.

"Is something bothering you, my child?"

The old woman stumbled before turning around to see exactly who was talking to her. It was a priest. He wore glasses and his eyes were light blue, his hair a starch gray from old age. Even at his apparent senior status, the old woman didn't truly believe that this man could be any older than her. Immediately, she felt insulted by the way that he called her "my child." At a younger age, the old woman would have cursed the man out and grabbed something from the altar to beat him with. In another point of her life, she may have actually killed him. That was when things had really gone bad— she wouldn't even try to do such a horrible thing anymore. All she could do now was to smile pleasantly from her wrinkled face and pull back her bonnet a little, just to be more polite to the holy man.

"Father," the old woman said respectfully to the man as she got off of her knees, grinning and holding her purse. "Why would you think that anything is wrong?"

"I could tell. I just looked at you praying down there and you looked very worried." The priest shook his head. "I'm sorry. How rude of me to intrude on you when you are praying."

"No, no, it's quite alright," the old woman said.

"If you want... I can tell that your heart is very heavy." The old priest smiled amicably. "If you want to, you can come to the booth and do a confession. It would make you feel better to get things right with God, and I can help you."

The woman looked to the side. "Well, you see, Father... for one, I don't feel comfortable doing confessions with you having seen my face."

The priest was taken aback, just a little, but he tried to hide it in the best way that he could. "Oh."

"Please don't take offense. It's just... the things that I have to let off of my chest. I never let it be known to... outsiders before. I have to get things right with God on my own. Sorry."

"I see. Maybe it would be okay if I asked you for your name?"

"I'm Maria."

"Maria," the priest nodded. "Well, tell me, Maria... are you Catholic?"

"I was raised Catholic, but, no, I'm no Catholic."

"Well... it's never too late to come back. The church will always embrace you with open arms."

Maria shook her head, staring at the man calmly. "For the things I have done and seen... for the things I have encountered...."

"Your heart will feel so much lighter if you can get rid of these things that weight your heart. It's not for you to handle. It's for God. Do you understand?"

Maria raised her brows and sighed. "I guess so, Father." Turning around, she looked back to the altar. "Now, if you don't mind Father, I would like to go back to praying."

The priest nodded. "Okay, fine. I understand."

The priest walked away and left Maria alone to pray. God, Maria thought, I thought he would never leave. Maria liked the atmosphere of the church and how it felt, but she could never trust priests. Not when she grew up seeing priests having secret relationships with mobsters and gangsters that dealt with crimes so unspeakable Maria wanted to throw up. No, she couldn't trust a priest to help her to get into heaven.

If there was a heaven.

At this time in her life, Maria had more fear for theology than ever. Out of all of the things that she had done, she didn't feel as bad for the murders. She didn't feel as bad for the arsons, or the robberies, or even the fights she used to get into with other women and mobsters alike. No, she feared what she had done sexually. She had fucked so many men, had escapades with so many lovers, and didn't care where she ended up sleeping at the end of the night sometimes. Her father's voice would sometimes pop in her head, scolding her and calling her a slut. It had been that way for the past few decades. She truly hoped that he wouldn't be one of the people she saw when she died.

"I always hated my father," Maria said with a sigh, interrupting her own prayer session and deciding that it was time to go. Grabbing her purse, she got back up and made her way toward the doors.

Did she really think that she was going to get out of all of this? Her mind was racing. No, she was probably just going to die as another old woman with hopes and dreams, lost in the wind. As soon as she stepped out of the church, she pulled out a cigarette and started to smoke away. She wanted to get rid of all of her fears—pretend that they weren't there. Hell had been pushed so heavily on her as a kid.

She thought about Sal. She thought about how he was the absolute opposite of her father. Even with his stern way of handling a gang, he had always been so sensitive and delicate with her, even loving. There was a submissiveness he had with her as well. Maria loved it. When she had left the gang, he supported her and wanted her to find a peaceful life. She went through a lot of pain after finding out that he had died of colon cancer only 20 years ago.

The day was supposed to be a simple visit to Sal's grave. That was the agenda at first. Maria couldn't be surprised with how she entered the church as well. Maybe she was trying to relive something—go through a sense of nostalgia in seeing the church she had been raised in. She hadn't told the old priest something she noticed while they were talking—she remembered the priest when he was a young man. In remembering that, she realized the man was about a decade younger than she was. Maria felt even more insulted.

Fuck this place, she thought as she put out her cigarette on the brick exterior of the church and started to walk off.

"Sisters, I officially call the Saint Maria meeting to an official opening!"

The Saint Maria club was a very small one. It was more of a sisterhood than a club, really. All of the women involved felt very close. They had been the wives of mob bosses, gang members, and street runners. Now, they were united under a number of goals—to make money, have sex, and control neighborhoods. They were empowered to take over whatever they could in the Big City, and they were all thankful to one woman for giving them the motivation—Maria.

No one knew Maria, personally. She lived a long time ago, so chances were that she was dead. At least that's what most of the mob women in the club were quick to believe. They doubted that a legend like her would have lived long after living in the Big City. No one really knew why she left. She was close to one of the biggest mobsters from the golden age, a man only remembered as Sal. Most of the members of his crime syndicate ended up being arrested or murdered. Some of them probably pretended to die only to escape the country. Faking death was apparently a big thing for gangsters that couldn't get out of the life, whether they were trying to get away from the police or get away from their own mob brothers.

The women were certain that none of them were looking to get out of the life. They loved their work. It was important for them to live in control, taking over the streets, getting what they needed by any means necessary. Nothing could slow them down. They had a high arsenal of guns and drugs. They were all professional businesswomen and killers.

They were also lovers. Each and every one of them. After their weekly meeting, they had extreme orgies with each other. No men were allowed. The way it usually started was the way that the meeting was ending that particular meeting.

The leader, Jessica, slammed down her gravel three times and stood up with a smile. "Okay, girls, the meeting has come to an end," she said before pulling off her top as her sisters cheered her on. She gave a cheeky smile as she showcased her breasts, throwing her bra on the head of one of the women. The woman with the bra on her head, Sonya, was already fingering herself, ready to get the party started. Standing up from her seat, Sonya walked up to Jessica and kissed her directly on the mouth. With her hands on the back of Sonya's ass, Jessica pulled the woman closer, their kissing session getting hotter and steamier while all of the other women found a partner to play with.

Sonya kissed Jessica as the leader pulled down Sonya's shirt, leaving her topless as well. With naked breasts, they rubbed against each other and shared perked breast nipples. Sonya slipped some fingers in the crack of Jessica's ass, starting to pump it inside of her fast and quick, licking her tongue against hers. Jessica had spread her legs, wrapping them around Sonya's body as she rubbed her back. Jessica's legs were so strong and Sonya could tell as she felt Jessica's calves rub against her.

Sonya and Jessica weren't the only ones having fun. There were four other members in their club, each one forming their own couple for the evening. Ericka was with Cathy. Sara was with Stefani. The girls never met up with the same girls in every meeting—they liked to switch off, keep things different, and enjoy each other in a variety of ways.

As Sony and Jessica kissed, scissored, and fingered each other, Ericka ate Cathy out for fun. Cathy arched her back as she held onto Ericka's head to her pussy, squeamish as she felt her cunt getting handled by her mob friend. The scent of cunt was everywhere, flooding the room mercilessly as the women screamed and moaned. Cathy almost lost control of Ericka's head but got back in a dominant role, holding the woman's hair and making sure she ate her pussy right.

As for Sara and Stefani, they didn't see fun in just one person being eaten. They did a 69 together, both of them teasing and eating each other's cunts. They tasted so good to each other, clean and wet, splashing into each other's mouths with each lick and drop. Their cunts were opening wide for each other, kissing their lips playfully. Before long, both of the women were moaning and crying, handling each other with fast tongues and strong hands refusing to let go.

The orgy continued for an hour. They couldn't be in the room for too long—they had money to make, business to handle. After it was guaranteed that every woman in the room had orgasmed at least twice, they were all good to go. Sweaty and hot, they pulled their clothes back on. With their hair disheveled and makeup messed up, the women took some deep breaths and composed themselves.

"Okay, girls, okay..." Jessica wiped her forehead and nodded. "We did well for tonight. Okay, we need to think about our new operation. Uptown needs to be ours in the next 48 hours. We've got the main boss running scared up there, and a lot of his enforcers are dead or left town. Let's do it."

Ericka raised her hand.

"Yes, Ericka," Jessica said, recognizing her friend civilly.

"Do you still want me to pay them a visit tonight?"

Jessica nodded. "Yes. I think they will get the message."

Ericka nodded. She was never one to ignore orders. None of them were. They were a union, a unit. What was good for one was good for all.

Five guys stood right outside of Murray's Fish Shop. It was a cold night on the northern Big City harbor, and they all wished that they could be home or somewhere else, sleeping with their wives or mistresses. Instead, they would have to stand there and keep their eyes open for approaching cargo.

"Why the hell did the boss want us to do this now?" one of the guys asked the others. "It's not enough that we were running shit for his fat ass all day today?"

"Shut up, you moron," one of the other guys said. He was the oldest of the group, about 54 years old, and the most experienced of the runners. He was also a bit upset that his status wasn't that much higher than theirs. "Whatever the boss says, we do. You got it, fuck face?"

"Fuck you!" the man said. He really got angry quickly. Gang life didn't seem the thing for him—he hated authority and that was why he joined, not knowing that he'd have to follow a boss or senior member the way one would follow a cop. "I don't have to listen to your shit. You're just one step over me, bitch."

"I should kill your bitch ass right now," the older man said as he stepped in the hothead's face.

Another one of the brothers got between the mobsters and protested against their actions. "Hey, guys, hey hey... slow the fuck down. What the hell are you thinking, man? We got to have unity for this. Think of the money—the money!"

"Yeah," the hothead said. "The money, jerk off."

The old man growled, "I'll jerk off you."

The hothead laughed. "Yeah. I bet you would, you homo!"

It stopped there. The older guy just stopped right then and there. He couldn't kill this guy without permission. He would just run his name by the boss later. He didn't like the younger ego heads barking at the vets. Oh well, he thought, just let him get off his own bravado. A smart man lies and waits.

As the men started to calm down, they looked up the road. There was an approaching light, obviously a motorcycle.

"You think a shipment truck is coming behind this fuck?" one of them asked.

"Not used to seeing people ride their bikes

around here," another one said.

It wasn't too soon before they realized that the bike hadn't come in peace. There was a loud BRRRRRRAT that sounded with bullets aimed at their direction. Two of them fell immediately, and as soon as the others had even tried to pull out their guns, they fell as well. Blood littered the scene. The men waiting to do a simple job were now dead and wouldn't see the shipment that was only ten minutes up the road.

The bike screeched to a stop.

"This is for the Saint!" the woman said before pulling out a hand grenade and throwing it at the fish shop.

As she drove off, the entire shop blew up. The bodies were on fire as debris fell, windows shattered and plaster ripped up. It would be another fifteen minutes before the cops would come. The shipment truck had already driven off by that time, alerting their bosses of what was going on.

"Captain... what exactly is happening on the north side of Big City right now?"

The captain of the Big City police force sighed as he looked at the press. "We are currently investigating, and as soon as we have information that is important for the public to know, we will let them know. Thank you."

Starting to walk off, the captain and his fellow officers groaned and sighed as they moved through a crowd of annoying reporters. The media was a strange thing for the police. In one sense, they often needed them in important cases, but in times like this, they could be a huge detriment. The last thing the police wanted the people of Big City to think was that a big tragedy was hitting the streets. Gang members and mafia members were always killing each other in the big city. That was just the way of crime in the city. It always had been.

"God," the captain started to say to the closest officer as they got into a squad car and drove away. "The media is always trying to blow this stuff out of proportion!"

The officer shrugged. "Sorry boss. What can I say? That's the way it is."

The captain sighed. "You know as well as I do that I understand that. We've both seen it. But we can't give in to this one. There can be panic. Look, you got any more information on this weird cult we heard about?"

"You meant the ladies that are into the Saint Maria?"

"Saint Maria... some sort of catholic thing or something?"

"No... she's an old Big City gang member. You know, boss?"

The man shook his head. "So they got more information on them? I'm surprised I didn't hear about this Maria thing."

"They're still uncovering information. The lady's statue is apparently in the mob museum. No one knows what happened to her. She just vanished from town one day.

She worked with that big-time mobster, Sal, back in the days. Some say that they were lovers."

"Well, that's interesting." The officer rubbed his chin. "So these ladies worship this gang woman?"

"Yeah. She's seen like some sort of suffrage figure or something. She made it possible for women to be respected in mobs down here as something more than a wife or a fuck buddy."

The captain shook his head. "So weird. Why would a woman want anything to do with something as dangerous as a mob?"

The officer laughed. "I guess it's the same reason any guy would want anything to do with a mob or a gang, boss. You know. Power. Money. Sex. Adventure. Some people just get off in being on the wrong side of the law."

The captain nodded. "Understandable. So, should we go and grab some donuts?"

"Let's, boss."

With that, the squad car had a set course.

"Fuck these bitches!" the boss of the northern mob shouted in his meeting.

All of the other mobsters were staring at the boss as if he were crazy.

The boss didn't appreciate the strange stares. He was losing his mind; he knew that. At the same time, he felt like it was all justified. There were many lives that had been lost in the recent massacres. Gangsters were wiped out. Friends were murdered in cold blood. Some soldiers had lost hope and committed suicide or skipped town. The northern mob was weak now. There was no way to get out in sight, and the boss felt alone.

"Why are you knuckleheads not doing anything other than gawking at me like fucking country chickens?" The boss banged his fists on his desk. "Do I have to do all of this shit by myself or what, you assholes?"

One of the mobsters couldn't talk it anymore. Seeing the boss go crazy like this was too much for him to take. "Boss, we've been doing everything that we can."

"We're low right now," the boss said. "Do you know what I'm saying? A lot of us are gone now. We don't have a lot of our people left. We can either give up right now or come up with a plan to get these bitches off our streets and execute them."

The front door of the northern mob meeting room was opened. Another mobster with a hat cast over his face and a trench coat walked in calmly.

"I found out where the women stay."

The boss looked at the man with rage. "You! Who are you? Were you invited here?"

Mobsters started pulling out their guns and aiming it at the man. They didn't trust outsiders.

"I was the man that was driving the shipment truck last night."

Everyone pulled back their guns and put it back in their waists.

The boss was frowning. "You left my men out on the curb to die?"

"They were already dead, dumbass. The building was on fire. What did you want me to do?"

"You come in here and talk to me like I'm some idiot off the street? Fuck you! Now listen to me, you slimy asshole... you better tell me what you fucking know or we're pulling our guns out and we're blowing your head off! And you better have the shipment we were supposed to get last night before those bitches blew our operation to high hell."

"Calm down, old man." The guy held up his hands calmly. "I dropped the shipment off at another warehouse this morning. I thought you would get a call about it, but they said you were in this meeting. That's why I came here."

The boss folded his arms. "Where are the ladies?"

"On the south side. If you have a pen, I'll give you the directions."

"I hereby call this meeting for the Saint of Maria club closed!"

The women started to strip for another long meeting together. Swapping bodies with each other, they started to finger and eat each other out, suckling each other's tits in a unified orgy. Instead of focusing on one partner for each two people, they would all help each other out. It was the least they could do in order to celebrate their biggest achievement from last night.

It was all well deserved. They had worked so hard to achieve what they were trying to do over the past few months. In a number of weeks, they had slowly brought the north side to their knees. They wondered how did a gang that once was composed of hundreds feel now that they were reduced to less than a dozen members. Also, how did they feel being brought down so quickly by just six individuals, mob rivals that were actually women? It was a big thing for them all, and tonight, there would be a lot of cunt licking, ass eating, and tit rubbing.

The room already smelled of sex. As the women pushed desks out of the way, they also pulled out foldable beds and started to get busy. They couldn't help but think that it would be a very busy night ahead of them.

It felt that way, at least.

They heard a gun sputtering outside.

"Get the fuck out here, you cunts!"

As the women's eyes widened in shock, they rushed for their weapons and did not even bother to get their clothes on. It wasn't long before they heard doors being broken into from other parts of their compound. They were going to have to get ready, and they didn't have a lot of time to prepare.

"It's the northern mobsters!" Ericka screamed.

Before they could react, their windows were being shot out. Gunshots were also coming down from the hallway. Immediately, the women pulled out guns and took to the windows and doors, shooting back.

The shootout got heated. It would go on for some minutes. Each side was ducking bullets, dodging and trying to intimidate each other with insults and taunts. In the end, however, the loud gunshots would only work to attract the sounds of sirens.

"Miss, would you like more tea?

"No, thank you," the old woman told the bartender.

Maria was in an old bar downtown. She had woken up early that morning and wanted to catch the highlights from the game last night. Hopefully, she hadn't missed too much.

Suddenly, a news flash came on the television. What came on astonished Maria. There were line-ups of mobsters, both men and women, who were arrested from a shootout the previous night. No one died. The women had all been naked when they were found. The men were the last remainder of a northern sect of a dying mob. The women were all members of the Saint Maria club. More details would be released later.

She wasn't surprised that there were still mobsters in the Big City. She was surprised that a group of women, probably perverts, had formed their own weird mob sect. They sounded more like a cult. Saints of Maria?

Maria guessed that they must have been Catholics or something. There was no possible way that she would be important enough for some crazies to make a group in her honor.

After downing her tea, Maria stuck around, hoping the game would come on quickly so she could get the hell out of Big City and leave it alone forever.

9 MACHINEGUN AND GAL PAL

Neo Metro was a tragic city. As a dark and dismal environment littered with shattered buildings and strange militaristic domes filled with robotic soldiers, the place didn't seem welcoming at all. If a human was seen, they were either a loyal member of the Utopian Army Brigade or they were a destitute pauper looking for food in the rubbish of trash cans standing on the sides of the streets. No one smiled unless they were taking sick delight in the violence of some beggar getting shot by a soldier. No laughter was heard unless it was at the expense of a new victim protesting against the Supreme Ruler. This was his perfect world and no one was safe from his grasp.

The Supreme Ruler was a tall man, a bit thick with muscle from his obsessive weight lifting though his legs were scrawny. He was constantly insecure about his balding head but swore he would never try to hide it by wearing a ridiculous toupee. No way—besides, he heard that the girls thought baldheads were hot, especially on a regal type of man. Why hide it?

No one could defy the Supreme Ruler—except for the two vigilantes that seemed to escape his wrath at every turn. With his only good eye, the right one, he would look at their pictures every morning. Scattered on his desk were photos of the nihilist punk hacker Gal Pal and her boy toy robot, the murderous android Machinegun.

Gal Pal was an undeniably beautiful woman, possibly in her early 20s, with purple-dyed bangs accompanied with shoulder-length pink hair. In her nose was a silver stud ring that shined from the left nostril. Both of her ears were lined with studs and loop ear rings as well. She was usually smoking a cigarette, wearing a short shirt that showed her hard-rock stomach and black gloves on her hands. Her jeans were tattered and worn. There was never a moment where she seemed to change over the years, maintaining her rebellious look without resistance.

Her extreme look didn't seem like too much of a contrast to her boyfriend's taste. The android had a very punkish style himself and could easily pass as a human if not for his metallic right arm. His hair was spiked with a green tint as the sides were short cropped and blonde. There was a facial tattoo covering his forehead with vulgar language—words like shit, fuck, pussy, cunt, eat dick, and other things seemed to stand out without any real meaning. There was a picture where he had his tongue sticking out at the camera with a spiked ring in the center as if screaming directly at the Supreme Ruler. Other pictures showed him brandishing guns proudly, throwing up middle fingers and even mooning the camera comically. Nothing was as offensive as the facial graffiti tattooed into his face; however, the Supreme Ruler hadn't made him for that. Machinegun had gotten those horrific words branded onto him when he had left. It wouldn't be surprising if Gal Pal had tatted them on with her own hands and needles. The Supreme Ruler always doubted that the words were meant to convey any hidden message. To him, the vigilantes were just evil and ignorant pests, a dangerous couple always posing a threat to his order.

"I've gotten rid of so many enemies," the Ruler explained to his secretary as he thumbed through the pictures. "I've crushed opposing nations that didn't want to be united as one world utopia. I've eliminated political pests of all shapes and sizes. Why do these two rodents seem to give me so much trouble?"

"What do you expect, boss? You're the one that made them what they are today." The secretary was typing away at an archaic computer as she smacked on her gum. She was a beautiful but dorky looking woman— just the way the Supreme Ruler liked his women. She had cat-style glasses with pointed tips near the handles and a mole over the left side of her lips. Her black short skirt showcased her slender legs as her breasts stood out full and luscious under her white buttoned top. "The woman was trained at one of your top hacker facilities and graduated the highest of her class. I know that just as well as you do—I was her classmate. And you made that robot to be your best. It's just unfortunate that you gave him a mind of his own."

"I hate them," the Ruler said with clenched fists.

The secretary shrugged. "It's Machinegun and Gal Pal. They're professionals."

The Ruler shook his head. "I've doubted them. Time and time again, I've underestimated their power. With everyone else, it's submit or be killed. But these two, they've killed so many of the troops I've sent after them."

"Can't really send anyone to handle what you should be handling yourself."

The Ruler looked up from the photos as he slapped some off of the desk. With an angered face, he walked over to the secretary and grabbed her by the throat, lifting her up from her desk as she shrieked. Her feet dangled in the air as the chair toppled over, her eyes looking into her boss's.

"Are you suggesting I just go after them when I have an Empire to run?" the Ruler asked angrily as he looked into the woman's eyes. "They've killed my best assassins! I'm a scientist and a ruler, not some damned cyber warrior!"

The secretary puckered her lips as she

closed her eyes. The Supreme Ruler kissed her, feeling the woman's heart melt instantly. He could never be angry with her long. She only said these things for his own good. Before long, he was bending the woman over on her computer. He didn't care if she ruined the file she was typing for him or not. This was how things usually went anyway. He would wake up, come to work, and get upset about his vigilante foes, knowing they were out there. Then, he would get so agitated that all he wanted to do was fuck. The secretary just said things that triggered him, that made him want to hurt her. Before long, they were getting animalistic.

"This is my last hurrah, isn't it?" The Supreme Ruler looked sorrowful for a moment. "My last stand. My empire is finished."

"Don't be foolish," the secretary said breathily. "Don't say such things."

This time would be no different. The Supreme Ruler had already thrown the woman's glasses on the ground, her shirt over her head, and her shoes against the door.

"Maybe I should just waste my time fucking you," the Ruler asked his secretary as he spread her now exposed ass checks. "Is that it?"

The secretary moaned as she looked as far behind her as she could from the side, her eyes filled with a yearning look. "But boss... we've got so much work to do."

It was too late. The secretary gave a loud

moan as the boss's cock inserted into her ass like a jet reaching the cockpit. Her hands grabbed the side of her computer as she looked at the screen. Fuck, she thought as she was getting fucked harder. The paper she had been typing for the Supreme Ruler was already getting messed up with long lines of garbled letters and symbols. She would have to fix that when they were done.

The Supreme Ruler held the woman's hips as she started to whine loudly from the cock pumping into her ass. He grinned; this was one of the perks of his job. He had taken over the planet a decade ago, made a utopia that outlined his ideas the exact way he wanted it. Still, he was a lonely person. He didn't really like people, which was why most of his employees were robots. It was just a shame that his best robot had to betray him.

Machinegun. The bastard. The Supreme Ruler gritted his teeth as he fucked the secretary harder and harder, grabbing her ass cheeks with strong gripping hands. I'll kill him, he thought over and over. I'll kill him. I'll kill him. I'll—

Each thought of death was accompanied with the secretary's moaning. She was whining as, occasionally, she would take a hand and finger herself. This wouldn't last long as she really needed a good grip from the hard ass fucking that she was receiving. She would reach out and grab the computer again. Her eyes were wet with tears. Smells of sex were getting stronger in the room.

The Supreme Ruler's teeth were gritted

tight as he looked down on the woman like a tasty morsel, trying to take his mind away from thoughts of death and destruction. How he would take the former woman that used to be one of his top hackers, Gal Pal, and put her on a stake for public display against any human that would want to defy him. How he would eventually capture his disloyal android Machinegun and shatter his metallic skull, recycling his parts for future weapons his other robotic denizens would enjoy. In the end, he would get his revenge. He would have his last laugh.

Until then, all he could do was fuck his way into a sense of being on top.

Gal Pal wasn't the type of chick to wait for the end of a sexual session in order to light up a cigarette. She would light it right then and there as she rode her robot man, her arms stretched out to the sky as she took a puff. Then, she would let her arms back down, pull out the cigarette and grip the android's strong shoulders, looking him eye to eye.

It always got Machinegun excited. Thank the robot manufacturers that he was created with a sex drive and a cybernetic dick. He could make Gal Pal orgasm five times in a row if he wanted to. At times, he just wanted to savor it, let her have fun as they fucked for hours and hours.

This time, they had a job to do, though.

They couldn't wait for long. He looked her in the eyes as he could see her admiring the green spikes of his artificial hair, looking at him with the same longing love that he felt. His thick cock was held in her cunt like a hand in glove, sealing their unspoken matrimony each and every time.

Machinegun was made in a time where cybernetics was taken to a higher level. The previous government had fallen in the midst of high unemployment and mad scientists running back and forth, trying to take advantage of corrupt politicians on their last leg. Wellington was the one who became successful. As a big-time scientist in the Big City, Wellington had convinced a worried and needy world that they needed his guidance, his help. In a matter of decades, he took over, destroying what was left of the previous world and uniting it under one umbrella—his umbrella. He became the Supreme Ruler. Machinegun was supposed to be his crowning achievement, his magnum opus in a sea of impressive but common robots.

Unbeknownst to Wellington, Machinegun would develop a mind of his own. He had no interest with being a small fry in an evil corporate "utopia." He would take the Supreme Ruler's hottest hacker with him.

It wasn't long before Machinegun and Gal Pal had built a legacy of their own. They had stood up against Wellington the Supreme Ruler, challenged his idea of a utopia, and fought his soldiers both robotic and human. Many had stepped up and tried to stop them. After four years of gun fights, car chases, and dodging explosions, they were still here. They refused to give up—ever.

Machinegun had always told Gal Pal that death would be the only way out, and they were set on one thing. They would never die until the Empire died.

Now, she was on his lap, giving herself to him as he gave himself to her. They were in love and nothing in the world could separate them. He held and played with her nipples as she sat on him, her thighs spread over his. How he would hate that this would have to end so soon, but there would always be other playtimes.

Machinegun often did this strange thing with his dick that no human could ever do. He would spin it, like a tornado, into his girl's cunt at a fast speed. That always got her screaming and making sensual noises in a wild frenzy of excitement. After only a few seconds, the spinning action of his robotic dick had her squirting in an undeniably powerful orgasm.

"Oh, baby!" Gal Pal screamed as he finished fucking her clit.

"Wow, babe," Machinegun said as he grinned. "That was fun. But we better get to work before anyone finds out we're on Wellington's bed."

Gal Pal pulled off of her boyfriend as she laughed. "Oh yeah. They would really be pissed! It's enough that we have to do what we have to do."

"We've waited years for this. The time has come." Machinegun sat up and started to move off the bed. "Let's get dressed and suit up."

The Supreme Ruler was groaning again. Only ten minutes ago, he had made his secretary cum as he joined her. The sensation was great and they were going for round two, on the floor as he fucked her pussy raw. Her wet cunt was dripping all over the carpet but he didn't mind. He played with her breasts as she screamed loudly, filling the office with the sounds of her amusement. Some books had fallen from the bookshelf, pencils and cups on the ground after being knocked off the tables.

After forgetting about paper work and tasks that needed to be done for the day, the secretary just moaned and whined, trying to concentrate so she could meet the ruler's thrusts with her own, helping him fuck her pussy. She hated to make him do too much work alone but sometimes it felt so good that all she could do was scream and squirm. Her thoughts were all focused on the Supreme Ruler—she would do anything for him. She really wanted him to have success at every turn, to crush his foes. She hated to see him unhappy and she always hoped that offering her body to him could help relieve him of the stress he felt. She wanted to make him more satisfied and joyful. Ever since hacker school, she had always wanted to be in the hands of the

Supreme Ruler. Gal Pal had always made her jealous, but now, she was the leading star in the Ruler's eyes. She would help him towards all of his goals.

Making a funny gasping sound with a long and final thrust shoved into the woman, the Supreme Ruler felt his last load shoot into her. It felt so good, so right. God, he thought, that was enough. He couldn't do a round three. They would really have to get to work.

The two of them were sweating and panting profusely on the floor when, suddenly, a knock sounded at the door. It did sound quite frantic.

The Supreme Ruler looked at the door's direction. "Um, yes. Who is it?"

"It's me, sir!" a voice said. It was just as frantic as the knocking had been. The Supreme Ruler recognized the voice instantly as one of his human sentinels that guarded the courtyard.

The Supreme Ruler sighed. "Not now, not now... I'm busy!"

"I'm sorry, sir, but whatever you're doing, you can't do it now! Machinegun and Gal Pal are on the premises, and—"

The Supreme Ruler nearly had a heart attack as he jumped up from his playmate. "What?"

The voice behind the door was trembling. "A-a-and they're headed this way!"

The Supreme Ruler's eyes widened. "Fuck!" He looked down at a shocked and worried secretary. "Didn't you hear that? Get dressed; we got to get the fuck out of here."

The secretary stood up immediately, going for her clothes. "Where are we going to go?"

"I have a place," the Supreme Ruler said without missing a beat. He would have to think quickly from this point on.

Machinegun and Gal Pal were running through a long hall, shooting up every robot and human soldier they saw on sight. Their foes seemed to be everywhere, trying to keep up with the speed of the two but failing at every attempt. Dodging bullets and diving from small bombs, they made their way deeper into the compound, taking out as many of the soldiers as they could.

"Keep up!" Machinegun said as he shot at the soldiers rapidly with his metallic gun. With the cybernetic bullets they produced, he never ran out of bullets. Soldiers instantly met their death as he aimed towards them, riddling their bodies with holes.

"Easy for you to say," Gal Pal said as she held guns in each hand, shooting as quickly as she could. She could see the frustration of the soldiers as they tried to hit the human vigilante, only to get blown away by her rapid firing. "You're a robot!"

"Fuck that," Machinegun said playfully. "Excuses, excuses!"

What a long hallway, both of them thought. They remembered it well, just as they had remembered the entire compound.

They had come armed and focused, ready to bring on the revolution they had planned for years. They always told themselves that they would come back and destroy Wellington's empire. They wanted to make him cower in fear before killing him. Now, they had their chance. After taking out much of his military and loyal combatants, they could feel the day of victory in their hands. They would take out the head of the empire.

Finally, the couple reached the end of the hall. Just like the courtyard, they had taken out the soldiers in the hall. Bodies littered the place with blood as bullets had been lodged in foreheads, eyes, abdomens, crotches, and all types of places. Destroyed robots were spewing electricity from metallic limbs as some of their eyes and faces still moved before phasing out, losing robotic consciousness.

"Piece of cake." Gal Pal smiled. "Care to claim our prize?"

"Let's do exactly that," Machinegun said with a smile as he opened a door for the woman. "You still remember the way?"

"Just as much as you do," Gal Pal said.

They went on to the next part of the compound, knowing that the Supreme Ruler was close. So close.

"Fuck! Can you open that door fast enough?" The Supreme Ruler yelled in panic as his last soldier tried to open the door to his underground chamber.

"I'm trying, sir, I'm trying!" The soldier cried as his body trembled all over, trying feebly to undo the lock.

"Hurry, please hurry," the secretary said, trying to stay calm as she hugged up against The Supreme Ruler.

"I'm trying, I'm try—" The soldier stopped involuntarily as POW! A gunshot to his head sent him falling against the door. His blood smeared against it as the secretary screamed.

Both the Supreme Ruler and the secretary looked behind them. Machinegun and Gal Pal stood behind them, holding their weapons up.

"End of the line," Machinegun said, as he looked The Supreme Ruler in his eyes.

The Supreme Ruler shook his head. "So you're here. Both of you. You plan to take me out, huh?"

"The man that made you?" the secretary chimed in.

"Shut up, bitch," Gal Pal said to the secretary. "This is between us and the big man."

"Small man is more like it," Machinegun said as he stepped forward. "We destroyed your army. Decimated it, actually. Now, it's your turn. A captain must go down with the ship."

The Supreme Ruler gritted his teeth. "You really believe that?"

"Yes," Machinegun said with a cocky grin. "A tyrant dies with his empire."

With his eyes fixed on the two vigilantes

like a hawk, the Supreme Ruler growled. "Very well, then, my son. Do your duty."

"I've waited a long time for this."

The secretary hugged up against the Supreme Ruler.

Suddenly, a loud shot rang out.

Machinegun felt on his knees, his robotic head nearly gone. It was mere shrapnel now, spewing electricity everywhere.

Gal Pal screamed as she dropped her guns immediately. She was horrified, hugging Machinegun as the electricity shot out of his neck in sparks. It wasn't long before electricity travelled through Machinegun's body, traveling through Gal Pal as her eyes widened. She was being electrocuted. Machinegun's body phased out, Gal Pal's grip loosed as she fell on the ground nearby her robotic man.

The Supreme Ruler looked to the edge of the room as he saw, from the open door on the other side, four soldiers standing there. One of them was a robot and the other three were human, blood covered on all of their clothes. Miraculously, they had survived, though obviously worn and exhausted.

Both the Supreme Ruler and his secretary walked up to the fallen bodies as the soldiers joined them. One of the soldiers knelt over Gal Pal as he felt for her pulse. Looking up to the Supreme Ruler, he said somberly, "I think she's still alive, sir. I feel a pulse, though it's weak. What should we do?"

The Supreme Ruler looked down at Gal Pal. His face of surprise and confusion soon transformed into a joyful face, his smile wide and white. "These heretics must be made an example of. Come, let's drag them to my leisure room."

Machinegun's robotic carcass was hung out for the public near Neo Metro's main gates for everyone to see. Hanging from a crucifix, the robot was headless, his metallic limbs rippled and defiled, lacking its artificial skin.

Wasn't that the one that betrayed the Supreme Ruler? That was the question that many of the utopia's citizens, both robot and human, would wonder quietly to themselves but never ask publically.

As for Gal Pal, she made a good whipping post in the Supreme Ruler's leisure quarters. Tied up in his chambers, the Supreme Ruler would beat her profusely. It made good foreplay for the Supreme Ruler and his now many secretaries. Besides, Gal Pal was realizing that she quite liked her new life at the Supreme Ruler's headquarters. It became even more enjoyable when her human brain was replaced with a new content and robotic one.

One day, near the main gates, a passing vagabond looked up before entering Neo Metro. Although his eyes may have been fooling him, he could have sworn he saw the robotic carcass twitch against its crucifix.

END

10 I LOVE VAMPIRES LOL

Maggie had always liked vampires. As long as she could remember, she had loved to see vampire movies. She never liked the glamorous vampires that looked like they could star in a drama magazine or land a spot on a soap opera. For Maggie, vampires had to be gritty, hungry, needing blood, and constantly looking for a new supply of vampire slaves to infect with their disease. Even though she was a fan of many horror creatures with many posters on her wall, nothing could stray her away from her first love of vampires.

With as many slasher films, paranormal movies, and historical pieces on Vlad the Impaler that Maggie had watched, she liked to pride herself as a horror expert. She always felt that way about herself, and even when she got to work in a theatrical store, she made sure that she made herself up as a vampire every day. It all came with the territory. The job required people to dress up but they could dress anyway they wanted and she came as a vampire. Even when the other girls in the store were dressing up as cartoon characters, fairy princesses, and movie stars, Maggie was dying her hair black and wearing her makeup caked on thick like some Victorian disaster. She would plaster fake blood on herself and keep on black attire, sneering playfully whenever she saw a cross or someone opened the door for some sunlight. She even avoided the sunlight, which was hard to do on a daytime job.

"She seems to take this job way too seriously," one of the coworkers told the boss. Of course, Maggie was in the back on her lunch break at the time. No one said anything to Maggie when she was around.

No matter which coworkers complained or got uneasy and wigged out at the fake vampire's presence, the boss didn't mind. As far as the boss could tell, the vampire character that Maggie dressed as everyday was bringing the store a constant flow of traffic, even when Halloween had long passed. More people than theater students and dress up junkies would stop by and buy something just to see the vampire girl they had heard so much about, impressive in the way she played her role even in ringing up the cash register.

"Maggie is a freak," another coworker said to the boss on a rainy day. Maggie was absent that day.

When Maggie was around, however, the coworkers would sing her praises and idolize her beautiful works.

"Oh, but you're so beautiful," the girls said as they stared her up and down, playing with her dark hair and looking at her shiny shoes. "You shouldn't change your look for anyone."

"I wasn't planning to," Maggie would say nonchalantly with a musing smile. "I never planned on it." How many times did she have to tell these women? It seemed like the same statements would come up every week.

Maggie wasn't ignorant to what was going on. She understood her reputation very well. As much as she got along with her boss and was able to hold up a positive rapport in the place, she knew that the people she worked with were bitter enemies. Even in being cordial with them, she would be damned if their secretively disruptive and hateful ways would take her away from what she loved— the theatrics of vampirism.

Secretly, however, Maggie did wish that vampires were real.

Every night, Maggie would retire to her humble home and sleep. She would have these dreams, intense dreams of being romanced by vampires. First, they would initiate her, feeding on her blood but not killing her. She would be chosen to share their disease with them: the one that kept them alive that makes them one with the living dead. As a nocturnal creature of the night, she would be given a new identity, feast with her new friends, and drink blood out of wine glasses. Her mind couldn't help but muse on what a glorious lifestyle it would be to be immersed, truly immersed, in vampire culture and not just a fantasy. She could feed on all of her enemies without converting them, giving them no hope but absolute death. She could destroy the world around her without a care for anything but the nightlife and unholy union, peace found in the graveyards and old mansions of the countryside. How much she loved this fantasy.

Then again, she would always wake up in that same comfortable bed. Her room would come back to her as she opened her eyes. Posters of her favorite movies would be scattered about on the wall as her radio alarm blasted the gothic music she had preset it to. God, she would think to herself, why can't I be dead?

Undead. In reality, she felt like death was her only reward that she could really look forward to, so she tried to be realistic. Still, in her heart of hearts, she knew that it was the undead life that she was looking for. She wanted to be eternal night, and yet she walked around in the day, pretending, wanting to be, and never getting what she truly desired. If anyone knew that the pretty girl with gothic leanings and a love for theater dreamed of suicide, they would be shocked. Even to her closest friends, Maggie always seemed like the one that had a natural zest for life. All the while, she really wished to kill herself. A powder white face wasn't enough. Dark eyelashes and red lipstick that was as red as blood didn't do it for her. She wanted her body to really be drained to the point of destruction, feel her skin staying in a constant cold shiver, and look into a mirror to see that she had no reflection at all.

"It's just a dream," Maggie would always tell herself before coming home from work, washing up, and getting ready to go to bed. "It's just a dream and nothing more." Then, she would go to bed and have her dreams, dreams that seemed so real in the night, yet so far away in the morning.

She wished her life wouldn't have to always be that way, and one day that wish came true.

The day started out as it usually did. Maggie came into work and heard the women around her singing her praises and giving her props for her well-designed attire for the evening. Maggie would just grin and see through their bullshit respectfully and in silence. She would work the cash register, help people around, and even take photos with her adoring fans that had heard so much about her in their last play or meeting. Either way, Maggie got through the day as she usually did, and when she got home, she decided she would have some time to play on the computer.

Maggie went online every now and then.

She wasn't in any way an addict. Mostly she would Google things and look up her favorite movie actors, movies, and vampire novels. She would keep everything that appealed to her organized in her bookmarks. She had many folders to organize websites in, folders with titles like vampire slashers, vampire murders, vampire rituals, and vampire cults. Sometimes she laughed to herself about how she would never have a vampire romance folder or a folder for pretty boy vampires. Yuck! She preferred women, herself.

Still, the woman had to wonder. Was romance such a bad thing with vampires? A vampire romance didn't have to be soft, touchy, or Hollywood, did it? Maggie thought back to the movies where she thought she had seen a vampire romance done really well. There were movies were she remembered people getting together and romping in pools of blood and feeding on spare vials of the stuff. Sometimes they would pass blood around as if they were downing bottles of vodka or liquor. Shortly after that, they were all ready to live the night wild. After sessions of fucking, unholy kissing, and feeding, they would protect themselves from the approaching day in coffins, only getting ready to have more fun the next day.

Maggie really wished she could live that way.

As she was searching for some new vampire websites, something really interesting came up. Staring at her as big as day when she was looking on a movie site, Maggie saw a banner that really appealed to her. The words of the banner read: "Session with a Real Vampire: Have Your Special Chat Today For Free!"

"Hmm..." Maggie said to herself as she scrolled away from it. "Probably a scam."

It probably wasn't, her mind thought. Just think, the opportunity to speak to a real vampire! She wanted to do it, but she knew how foolish it was to really think she could talk to a real vampire. "Still, what would a little fantasy hurt," she thought to herself. Was it wrong to speak to somebody that was probably paid to speak to vampire enthusiasts all day? No. She would be getting her fantasy fix and whoever did the work would get their money that they probably needed. Still, it kind of worried Maggie how the website said it was free on the banner. She was sure that it was a scam, just sure of it! Maybe there was some small print she couldn't see or a time limit. After 5 minutes, she might be paying out of the yin yang. Those actors had to get paid somehow, and she doubted that their employer was so generous to hire these people and then pay without any revenue coming to their site. Maggie couldn't look away from the banner, though. It was just too enticing. Either way, she needed this time. She had to get exactly what she wanted.

Maggie clicked on the banner. Instantaneously the website came up with a flashing light. Blood seemed to drip and flow in the graphics of the screen before a little box asking for a username and password came up. "Welcome," she heard the website's programming say in a gravelly voice as some old horror punk song played on the speakers. "A human's life is behind you now. Tune in and drop out... with our vampires."

"Fuck, I don't have a password!" Maggie said out loud to herself. "I don't want to register for anything."

Who cares, she thought? She didn't even see a button to register for an account. Oh well. She just typed a funny name for herself, MaggieNeedsABite, and typed in a silly password. PleaseImHorny.

"Haha," Maggie laughed as she clicked the enter button.

Boom. She was in. It happened so quickly and Maggie was truly astonished. There was even a little avatar for her with her picture on it.

"What the?" Maggie became fearful as she reached for the back out icon on the browser.

Suddenly, the browser disappeared. And boxes and places to type disappeared as well. Before she knew it, Maggie was staring at a huge chatter's avatar that seemed to cover the whole screen. The avatar was of a gorgeous but malicious looking female with dark hair and truly pale skin. Her gaze was penetrating and possessed no natural colors that Maggie was used to seeing. The woman was so beautiful and yet she freaked Maggie out at the very same time. Such an avatar seemed to pierce deeply into Maggie's soul, connecting like a parasite as Maggie was both fascinated and disgusted at the same time.

"Welcome, human," a seductive and sexy feminine voice said from the computer.

Maggie was shocked, surprised even. Was this a voice chat? The only few times she had chatted online, it had been through the text options. Even then, she was only chatting with other horror nerds that she doubted were attractive at all. Voice chat, wow! Maggie realized how much she needed to catch up to the times.

"What's the matter," the voice said again. "Are you scared?"

Maggie stumbled for a second as she tried to compose words to say. "I.. um.. hello."

"Hello to you, dear."

Suddenly, the avatar vanished. Showing itself on the screen this time was something completely different. Maggie saw the woman, but this time, she was certain that she was seeing her in real time. This was no photograph or avatar. The woman wore all black, her hair just as dark as her clothes, and her big and juicy boobs were pushed up, as if to entice whoever saw them. She smiled calmly as a beauty mole placed perfectly on the left side of her lips. God, Maggie thought to herself. The lady looked like Cindy Crawford—the evil Cindy Crawford. To make things more dramatic, she was surrounded by what looked like an underground dungeon.

Maggie was truly at a loss for words. "I... uh..."

The vampire woman leaned forward as she stared into the camera. "You wanted to see a real vampire. Well, dear, here I am. I answered your prayers. We can talk about anything and everything you would want to know."

Maggie smiled, though she was nervous. "Well, sure, thanks."

The woman pressed her fingers against her lips. "You're pretty."

Maggie lifted her brows. "You can see me?"

The woman laughed a bit as she moved back to sitting regularly. "Of course, I can see you! Just as you can see me, Maggie."

Maggie didn't even bother to ask how the woman knew her name. Oh wait, Maggie remembered, I typed it in my username, duh.

"I'm Natasha. But I love it if you call me Natasha the Vampire or Mistress Natasha."

"Okay... Natasha the Vampire."

Natasha sighed and rolled her eyes. "I was hoping you would go for the second option, really."

The women talked for quite a long time. Once Maggie got loosened up, she could ask her all sorts of questions she may have been afraid to ask in the beginning.

"Are you guys really scared of crosses or hurt by them?" Maggie asked innocently.

"No," Natasha said firmly. "We do not

discriminate against religion. Some of our vampires are Christians. They sleep in Christian graveyards. I am particularly agnostic myself."

Well, that's a weird answer that I didn't expect, Maggie told herself honestly.

Maggie couldn't help but admire the woman's look, her face, her breasts, and her smile as she spoke. Natasha was so beautiful. Maggie wished that she could look that good. People always told her she made a pretty vampire when she dressed up, but that wasn't the same thing. Natasha's skin was naturally drained of any blood. She was pale for real. Her eyes were darkened from a lack of sunlight. Her lips sccmed to be teased with real blood. Even in her hypnotic energy, she radiated a sexiness that was irresistible, dark, and brooding with power. God, Maggie thought, if only she could have a tiny iota of what Natasha had. If only she could have a chance at being the real thing.

Natasha stroked her hand in her hair as she continued to instruct Maggie on the real ways of the vampire. "So Magdalene, you don't mind if I call you Magdalene, do you?"

"Um, no, of course not," Maggie said, though hearing the weird name kind of confused her. "Though it does sound pretty Christian or Gnostic."

"Thanks. I think it sounds rather... Gothic too, don't you think?"

Maggie's eyes perked up. "Yeah. You're right. It does sound rather Gothic. I like it."

Natasha leaned forward and looked Maggie into her eyes. Teasing her lips with a tongue that seemed to never wipe away her lipstick of blood, Natasha asked, "Maggie, don't you want to be a vampire?"

Maggie froze. "Well, I, uh–"

"I know your desires, woman. Don't lie to me." Natasha tapped her cheek delicately with the nail of her index finger. "You can't go your entire life hiding from your dreams and desires, girl. A human doesn't have all eternity to contemplate things, but I assure you, a vampire can."

Maggie pulled at the collar of her top. It was getting extremely hot in the room all of a sudden. "Well, isn't it kind of... I mean, don't vampires lead a hard life?"

Natasha laughed boisterously.

"I mean, as we were talking," Maggie continued, "You did confirm that you can't go out in the sun."

"But, Magdalene, you hate the sun!"

"Well, yeah, I like the night... but kind of for pretend, you know? Vampires were, I mean, they were just like a fantasy. An escape from my life that I kind of hate, you know? They motivated me and kept me going."

"But you don't have to live this life the way that you do, Magdalene. You can be free and join your sisters of the night. Of course, I will be your mistress and the main woman that you stay with. Understand?"

Maggie noticed that she had been wet for quite a long time. Her sexual energy only increased when she heard Natasha's demand that being a vampire meant that Natasha would be the main vampire in her life. The thought did intrigue her, forever though? She didn't know... it felt so right at the moment, though.

"You'll just be starting out, a fledgling. But I'll train you. I will raise you up and make you the best damned vampire you could dream of being. You know you want it. Just say yes."

Maggie shook her head. "I don't know. I just–"

"Have to go back to the job you have? Be surrounded by the people that hate and ridicule you? Deal with being just another pretty face that pretends to be vampire? No, my dear, you deserve to be the real deal." Natasha breathed in deeply. Suddenly, her energy's feeling increased. "Feel me, Magdalene."

Maggie started to shiver a bit.

"When I walk into rooms," Natasha stated, "men get nervous. Some get nauseous. Others fall entirely in love. I either get extreme fear or extreme adoration. Then I kill. I drink blood. I swim in blood and bathe with it, and then I have sex. I am immortal."

Maggie fanned herself. She felt as if she had heard a speech or a performance by a powerful senator or politician.

"Just. Say. Yes."

Suddenly, Natasha's hand was reaching out of the screen.

Surprised, Maggie reached out and touched Natasha's hand. She stared into Natasha's smiling face for seconds as she swooned.

"Yes," Maggie said. There was no turning back now.

"You will not regret this, my sweet," Natasha said.

Suddenly, Natasha's hand let go of Maggie's. Her arm withdrew back into the computer as Natasha smiled. From there, the computer shut off completely.

"What the hell?" Maggie said as the screen went black and the soft sound of the computer ended.

"Don't look too hard," Natasha said from behind Maggie.

Maggie turned around to see the beautiful woman, in the flesh. Wow, she was even more beautiful in person. Her dark hair fanned behind her, a slender body with thick breasts, and hips that enticed Maggie calling her. With her hypnotic eyes, Natasha stared Maggie up and down like she was a morsel.

"You're so pretty," Natasha said with a grin. It was then that Maggie noticed Natasha's fangs. She was surprised that she hadn't noticed them before. Was this really real?

"You're here," Maggie said. "And it's true. You're a vampire."

"Yes. And soon you will be."

Natasha stepped forward, closer to Maggie. She pressed her hands on Maggie's knees as Maggie still sat in her chair. Natasha licked her lips.

"Well, human girl," Natasha said calmly. "Aren't you going to kiss me?"

Maggie felt her panties completely soaked

as the vampire woman leaned in, kissing Maggie romantically. As she held Maggie's chin, she pressed her lips against Maggie's lips, pressing against them softly and then fully taking control. Natasha stuck her tongue into the woman's mouth. She flicked the tongue around and was excited when Maggie found the courage to flick her tongue around as well. Even though Maggie had always been secretly into girls, Natasha could tell that this was her first time with a real woman—a real vampire woman, at that.

Pulling out of Maggie's mouth, the vampire woman pressed her nose against Maggie's neck and sniffed her scent in. "You smell so good. So fresh."

Maggie was blushing. For the first time in a long time, she actually liked a compliment that she received from someone else. She didn't feel any ulterior motive in it. There was a true union, a bond, even before any feeding took place.

The feeding started, however, and the initiation began. Natasha sunk her strong jaws into Maggie's neck. It caught the woman girl by surprise, and she gasped as the sharp jaws punctured her skin, but after that, she sunk into Natasha's arm. After that initial moment of surprise, Natasha was fine again. She could feel a bit of blood dripping from her neck and staining her clothes. Her passionately hot sexual energy was tempered with a coolness that swarmed over her skin. She held onto Natasha's back as she let her drink from her.

"Oh, mistress," Maggie said softly.

Natasha pulled back her hair as she looked into Maggie's eyes. Her next goal was to get Maggie completely naked, as the new initiate was a little weak from blood loss. With a superhuman strength, Natasha picked up Maggie in her arms and started to carry the woman upstairs. As if she had the house mapped out in her mind, Natasha took Maggie directly into Maggie's room. She laid the dying human's body on her bed, watching her being reborn through death as she peeled off the woman's clothes. Natasha was quite pleased with the size of Maggie's breasts. She flicked and pinched the nipples and rubbed and bounced the tits with enjoyment and pleasure as she smiled happily. After she had gotten Maggie comfortable on top of the bed, Natasha started to strip as well.

Even as Maggie felt her body becoming paralyzed and immobile, she could see Natasha's naked top and face as she stripped down, even the top of her ass. God, the vampire was so gorgeous! Maggie felt her paralyzed body dripping all over the bed. It was too much to hold to herself. She truly felt herself ready to give all of her energy to her new mistress.

Natasha smiled and teased as she walked over to Maggie, moving her hands through her hair as she spread her legs on top of the woman, pressing her cunt against Maggie's.

"And now, Magdalene, my sweet muse..." Natasha said with a grin. "Mistress gets to play."

Maggie moaned from her lips as her body had become completely cold.

The play began. Maggie bent down and ate the woman out. Stabbing her tongue into that vulnerable cunt, Maggie stabbed at it like she was at a picnic. Her touch was fiery, powerful, and ripped through Maggie like a whirlwind. Maggie truly felt dead, as if she was a corpse. She could just lay there as Natasha ate her out, the fingers of Natasha playing on Maggie's skin like a piano or violin. As she rubbed the woman's skin and felt her smooth complexion loosing color, Natasha smiled with pride. Yes, only in a couple of hours, she had won the human over.

Natasha fingered herself rapidly as she ate the human woman out. This would be the end of Maggie's life as she knew it. Hell, it was already over. No more grouchy coworkers, no more bullshit jobs, and most important of all, no more pretending. Through the powers of the internet and a chat room, Maggie's life had been saved from mere mediocrity and boredom. Maggie had gained the right and the potential to find her true self, the vampire within, that she had always wanted to be. With the flicking of a fast tongue, Natasha was bringing Maggie back—not to life, but to the undead.

Resurrection had taken its steady but quick process. Maggie was already moaning quite loudly. Her limbs were stirring. At first, she could move her toes, feeling her cunt getting eating out like a 5-course meal. After that, Maggie felt her back loosen. She could lift up. She made room for her mistress on the bed so that she could eat out Natasha too. They formed a perfect 69, holding each other's asses and feasting for what felt like hours. Their pussies were so ripe and wet, blessed with strong, enticing scents. Before long, Maggie would be climaxing.

She did climax. Magdalene never thought that vampires could orgasm.

Natasha spun up on the bed to stare face to face with Maggie. She moved her hand playfully in the undead girl's hair. "So, my dear... shall we go out for a blood shake with blood on the side?"

A humored Magdalene could hardly hold back any laughter. "LOL!"

11 HINT, HINT, HINT YOU IDIOTS!

How much did a girl have to say already? It was Kelly's second date with Brad and she wondered if he had ever been with a fast girl before. She wondered if the guy was really religious or just fucking clueless. Here they were, uptown with a nice dinner, and she was trying to give him all the signs. At moments, she kept re-crossing her legs, batting her eyes, puffing out her breasts, and whatever she could think of.

Was the guy gay? Kelly would lie if she didn't say that she was starting to get pissed off. Brad was just blah blah blahing about his days playing football in college. Kelly didn't have the heart to tell the guy that she didn't really want to hear what he had to say. She knew it would be mean and hurt his heart. So, instead, she just sat there, nodding her head and entertaining him, batting her eyes and twirling her hair.

The restaurant was a little nicer than what she was used to. Kelly liked to go to the seedy parts of the town. She enjoyed dancing, going out and getting fucked up off some drinks, shaking her ass, and showing off her tits to the wild boys. Even though that had been fun at one point in time, she was convinced that she had changed her ways. No more running around the town, sharing her cunt with the local guys that didn't have a job or their shit together. No way. She was going to go for the good guys— the guys her mom had always told her to get with. The ones with good jobs. The ones with money. The ones that went home early, said their prayers, and ate their vitamins. The good guys.

God, Brad was still rambling. Reliving his old days with zest and glorious recounting, it was as if he wanted to pull Kelly right into his dead world. Wake up, nerd boy, Kelly thought as she grinned and nodded. Those days are gone.

Was it bad to put out on the first date with a good guy? Kelly had heard that it was. Well, what about the second date? She was so confused and ignorant to this whole dating thing. All she knew was fucking. In fucking, you didn't have to listen to rambling, talking, or chuckling or even have to eat a damn meal unless you were guzzling cum on your knees.

"So then he passed me the ball," Brad said as he continued on with his millionth story (or at least Kelly thought it was the millionth. She had lost count). "And I'm looking around like why the hell is nobody covering me? I see the whole team coming for me. So I don't really have any time to think, you know? So I'm running. 10 yards, 20..."

"That's nice, dear," Kelly said as she twirled a finger in her hair. "I like fields, yards even. I get a lawn magazine in the mail sometimes. I need to renew my subscription though." Pointing behind her, Kelly said, "Hey, do you mind if we go to the bathroom and...." Looking around to make sure the coast was clear, Kelly picked up a celery stick on her plate and simulated fellatio with it, trying to give Brad a hint.

"Oh, you need to go to the bathroom? Sure, Kelly. Go ahead. I'll wait for you."

Kelly laughed. "Oh, I don't need to go to the bathroom by myself. You should come as well."

The guy blinked. "Um, that's strange. I've never gone to the bathroom with someone before, let alone a girl. Are the bathrooms even unisex?"

Kelly shrugged. "I mean we could just go in the guy's bathroom. Those things have stalls most of the time, right? I mean they usually do when I go in there."

Brad blinked in surprise. "Wait a minute... You aren't suggesting that we... I mean I, a guy, and you, a woman, go into the same bathroom?"

"Well, yes. Yes, I am."

"Well, honestly, Kelly, if you're that afraid to use the bathroom by yourself, you might need to see a psychiatrist. I've heard of these abandonment phobias and—"

"Goddamn it, Brad! I'm trying to give you a blowjob in the bathroom."

Brad stared back at the woman, blinking calmly without missing a beat. He placed his chin against one of his fists in deep thought as he tried to understand the term the woman said. "A blowjob. Is that like blowing a balloon by any chance? Well, if you got balloons, you can blow one up right out here. I don't think anyone would mind."

Kelly slapped her hand against her forehead. "Brad...I'm not trying to blow a balloon. Look, if you come to the bathroom, I can show you exactly what I'm trying to do right now."

"I don't understand. You don't have anything to be ashamed of if you're with me. Why can't you show me here?"

"Believe me, baby. I can't show you here. I want this to be absolutely right for us. It can't be right if we do this out here. Now, you follow me and I'll show you what you've been missing out on all your life."

"Well, okay. But I hope you're not trying to kiss me. I don't kiss too early in dating."

"I don't kiss, babe."

Kelly stood up from her seat and started to walk towards the male's bathroom, inspecting to make sure the coast was clear. Her date followed her obediently. When they opened the bathroom door, they saw it was a one-seat bathroom with a sink and mirror.

Just perfect, Kelly thought to herself.

"Make sure you lock that door," Kelly said

as she saw her date close the door behind him.

Brad locked the door and then turned around to look at Kelly. He was still confused, his eyes like those of a puppy dog. "I don't understand, Kell. Why would you want me to be in here with you? I don't feel right watching a woman use the bathroom."

Kelly sighed again as she dropped to her knees. "Just shut up. I don't want to hear you say another word until I am finished showing you exactly what a blowjob is."

Brad listened obediently, a bit puzzled as to why Kelly was kneeling with her head in front of his crotch.

Suddenly, Kelly pulled down Brad's zipper on his pants.

Brad gasped. "Kelly!"

"Shhhhhh...." Kelly pulled the pants down to Brad's shoes. She saw that his underwear had a funny design of bears on it. What a dork, she thought as she pulled the underwear down a bit, revealing Brad's cock and balls.

"Oh my God," Brad said in shock.

Kelly was pleasantly surprised to see that a nerd like Brad had a reasonably big cock with a relative size of balls hanging under it. "Oh wow, Brad. Looks like I may have an early birthday." Kelly pointed and rubbed a finger under the cock.

Brad laughed as Kelly touched his cock. "Wait a minute, Kelly. What are you doing? That tickles. Come on, stop..."

Kelly continued to rub the cock before it started to stand erect like a soldier. Come to mama, she thought as she started to rub the man's balls as well. She was so enticed just by the look of the cock as it stood up. Before long, her juicy lips were opening and enveloping the cock calmly.

Brad started to eye the door crazily. He was afraid of so many things at once. For one, what the hell was this lady doing with his private parts in her mouth? He surely didn't see this on any episodes of Randy Miffet. "Oh God, Kelly... this is... I'm sure we shouldn't be doing this."

Kelly pulled up from the cock, her lips drooling over Brad already. She looked up to Brad with a scowl. "Brad. Now what did I tell you? I don't want to hear you until I'm done. Now will you please shut up?"

Brad pouted. "I'm... I'm sorry—you're right. I'm being bad."

Kelly nodded. "Why, yes. Yes, you are. Very bad. Now shut the fuck up and let me do this for you." Bending back down, Kelly pulled her lips back over Brad's cock and started to suck it.

"Oh God," Brad said. This time, he said it without a sound of worry or fear. There was a sound of pleasure that was vibrating through his voice.

Got him, Kelly thought as she continued to suck the cock with hot delight.

"Oh... God...." Brad leaned back against the bathroom door as Kelly continued to suck him off. "Oh God, hallelujah. Yes, amen. OH God." He looked down to see Kelly's head going up and down, up and down like some of those bobble heads he had gotten from church. From up there, she kind of looked like she was playing a sport or going for some kind of goal. "Go for the gold, girl."

"I will, daddy," Kelly said as she pulled up a moment to talk. "You'll shoot cum all over the place."

"Huh? Wait a minute. What's cum?"

Kelly ignored the bumpkin as she bent right back down over his cock and continued to suck him off with her best motions. Her lips were so tight around his cock and she was getting the dick all lubed up in her spit. It felt good in her mouth and she was already feeling the cock penetrating her throat. Damn, she thought. For a first timer, the guy could really go inside of her. She decided to help the guy a bit, feeling sorry for him as she grabbed his hands and forced him to place them on the back of her head. Helping him push down on the back of her head, she was proud with herself when she noticed him pushing her head down without her assistance. With that, she could take her hands back down to the guy's balls and play with his sac as she sucked him off. God, she thought, he tastes pretty good. Kelly wasn't used to tasting guys that seemed to wash themselves. Was this what nice guys were always like?

"Oh God, please Kelly, whatever you're doing, don't stop!" The guy moaned and groaned as the woman sucked him off. He had never felt anything like this before and something about it scared him. Was this the thing he had always heard of to be supposedly special for marriage?

Kelly had to admit to herself that she was pretty confused. She had never heard of a guy that played football at any point in his life being confused or ignorant about sex. She had had sex with the entire football team of her college at one time in her life. That was a lot of fun and she could remember being drunk as fuck. Knowing her at the time, she was probably fucked up on other things at the time too. Oh well, she thought. At this moment, she was breaking a nerd in, making him know the beauty of beautiful cock sucking. Maybe that was all that she needed to concentrate on for the moment. She didn't want to get distracted. She really just wanted to taste his cum in her mouth. The moment she had that, she could feel good about herself. Even though she didn't want to be seemingly conceited, she knew she had always been pretty proud of her sexual prowess.

"Why, Kelly... why are you doing this?" The guy was pushing Kelly's head hard on his cock now. He was undoubtedly fucking her face now, probably unaware of the force he was using. That was okay since Kelly liked it anyway.

"Mmmph!" Kelly responded. "Mmphh!"

"Oh God, oh God, oh God!" The nerd held his ground as he leaned against the door, trying not to fall over from how good everything felt. He could nut all over the woman's face. Still, he had to compose himself.

Kelly thought about how she had to

compose herself too to make this kind of special since her sexual needs already blew a nice and quiet evening with a goody two-shoes. No, she couldn't just foolishly let this dork shoot cum all over her face like a clown. She had to make it special.... She had to.

Splat! Like a cream pie, as Kelly pulled back from the cock to make sure she hadn't sucked it too hard, the blow hole of the cock shot semen all over her face. God, how embarrassing! The guy had probably never seen his cum before, which was pretty pathetic for a thirty-year-old like him. She didn't blame him. The guy went to a religious school and grew up in the country. What more could she expect?

"God, Kelly, what is that!"

Kelly chuckled. "It's cum."

"Oh...oh my God. I'm so sorry, Kell. Really. I didn't mean to."

Kelly scoffed loudly, brushing the cum from her face and eating up. "That's what you're supposed to do, lover boy. Shoot that cum in my face. I like it."

"Really?"

"Yes. Any pro like me loves that shit."

"Kelly, language!"

Kelly sighed.

"I'm...I'm sorry. Look...whatever you did, that was so strange. I liked it. A lot. Um..."

"Yes?"

"Kelly? Well, would you marry me?"

Kelly chuckled as she stepped up from the floor. Taking a napkin, she wiped her face as she looked the guy in his eyes. "Well,

I'm sorry, Brad, but I'm a woman of standards. What we did just now—well, that leaves us disqualified for marriage."

Brad looked like he was about to cry. "Wait a second. What do you mean? I thought we were bonding!"

"Well, yeah, we were! But here I am, being a slut and corrupting such a good guy like you.... Look, I'm trying to turn a new leaf and the guy I'll marry. Well...as I was sucking your dick, I thought about how I need to find a guy more like you before I did what I did to you. Someone that doesn't know about stuff like what I did to you. A guy that I can hold out with before marriage. But now, sorry. It won't work. Uh uh. No way."

"Oh... Well, maybe you can call me."

Kelly giggled. "Good night, Brad."

Kelly opened the bathroom door and walked out of the bathroom. Brad walked out of the bathroom right after the woman, speechless as he watched her pick up her purse and walk out. He watched as her ass swished behind her. He had never noticed how beautiful her ass was before, even when he first met her at the football game. Oh well, he thought. That was fun while it lasted—more fun than he had ever dreamed of.

Pulling out his wallet, Brad looked at the uneaten food that was sitting at his table. He saw a waitress walking by and raised a hand. "Check, please?"

CRBO

Kelly thumbed through her phone

numbers that she had accumulated in the last couple of months. God, she had met so many guys. She did have a lot of choices with what she could go for at the moment. Maybe she would find a really good one this time—one just as rich as Brad but with a little more will power. She thought she could do it. It would just need some time and focus.

Finally, she found him. He was a handsome guy; she could remember as she stared at the number. His name was Peter. Haha, she thought. Peter.

"Okay, Pete," Kelly said as she started to dial the number.

"Gee, Kelly, thanks for calling me back. I thought that night at the convention would be the last time I would see you."

Kelly was dressed nicely in a purple dress with matching high heels as she held Pete's hand and walked with him after dinner. God, she was glad that she hadn't gotten all slutty at dinner this time. She had composed herself and, honestly, she was pretty proud of herself.

Peter was taking Kelly back to his place to talk a little. He was kind of clueless as to why Kelly suggested that they spent the rest of the night at his place—he didn't really find it that formal. Kelly didn't know why she had suggested it either. She said that she just really wanted to watch this DVD with him; she had the movie in her purse.

God, what an idiot, she thought to herself. Just don't give out, you slut. Whatever you do, don't do the same damn thing.

"What kind of movie is this?" Peter asked. "Is it that new blockbuster that just got released on video? God, I hope so."

"You'll see," Kelly said as she held onto Peter's hand. She really hoped that she could change the topic when they got to his place. She had completely forgotten in her idiotic blunder that the video she was suggesting they would watch was a porno movie.

She could tell that Pete was a good guy, too. She didn't want to corrupt him. Peter had been working on humanitarian efforts for quite a while, doing both paid work and nonprofit. He was also extremely religious, which Kelly had made one of her new requirements for the guys she was looking for. When she had asked Pete about sex on the phone, the man said, "Yeah, I can meet you at six. Or seven or eight." Perfect, Kelly decided.

"Oh, wow," Kelly said as they approached Peter's house. "Peter, your house is so big!"

They stood on the outside of Peter's house. There were three floors to the house and it had an interesting architecture. The guy's neighborhood had a lot of interesting houses as well. Kelly reasoned that they all must have been loaded as fuck.

Peter opened the door and escorted his date into his house.

"Welcome to where the magic happens," Peter said.

"Magic?" Kelly asked cautiously.

"Yeah. Movie magic. I got a special big screen in the front room."

Phew, thought Kelly.

The lovebirds walked into the front room. It was like a dream to Kelly. She was used to back rooms and glory holes. This place had a lot of class—there were chandeliers, cool bookcases covered with religious literature, and beautiful fantasy paintings. The guy was interesting. He had lots of interesting furniture everywhere.

"This might be a great place to fuck," Kelly accidently said under her breath as Peter adjusted his television and DVD player.

"What was that, Kelly?" Peter asked curiously.

"Huh? Oh, nothing!"

Peter had finished plugging in everything. Sitting down on the couch, he watched Kelly as she walked to the TV and reached into her purse.

Think of something, Kelly thought. God, I can't show him a porno! Think, think...

"Oops!" Kelly reached into her purse and pulled the DVD out of its case. "This DVD is all scratched up!"

"Oh, no problem!" Peter stood up and started to walk towards Kelly. "I got a DVD cleaner—"

SNAP! Suddenly, Kelly had broken the DVD into two pieces. "Oops! I'm sorry. I guess the DVD was really fragile with those scratches cutting so deep."

"Oh, wow," Peter rubbed his chin. "That's too bad! I was really looking forward to watching your DVD, Kelly. Oh well... I'm sorry."

"No!" Kelly rushed into Peter's open arms and pressed her head on his chest. "Now, what do you have to be sorry about?"

Peter looked at Kelly surprisingly, not really knowing what to do. His arms slowly and awkwardly enveloped the woman close to him. "Oh, I'm sorry. I don't know. I guess I thought differently than I thought about these things. I mean, I thought I had accidently startled you standing up and maybe that's why you accidently broke the DVD."

"Oh, Peter, you're such a sweetheart." Kelly kissed Peter on the cheek.

Peter instantly started to blush. "Well...golly gee."

"You're so cute." Kelly chuckled. "I really wish that I could thank you."

"Oh, there's no reason to thank me. I mean, why?"

"Well, you're kind of like a knight in shining armor. So protective and letting me come into your castle. I could really get to enjoy here. What do you think, babe?"

"I guess that would be nice after we get to know each other more. Who knows what the future holds."

"Yes, who knows," Kelly agreed. Looking into Peter's eyes, Kelly grinned. "You know what I would really like you to do? Maybe this is how I can thank you."

Peter looked confusingly at Kelly. "How?"

Kelly grabbed Peter's hand and slapped it on her ass.

Peter blushed. "Oh...my. Um, Kelly, what are you doing?"

"Letting you feel my ass." Kelly grinned as she helped Peter squeeze it. "What do you think of it?"

"Well, it's quite, um, flabby?"

Kelly frowned.

"Nice and flabby. I like it."

Kelly grinned.

"You know," Kelly continued, "there are lots of fun things that you can do with a flabby ass like mine."

Peter raised his brows attentively. "Really?"

"Yes, baby. And you know what they say. More cushion for the pushin'."

"Well...I guess I could always use more cushions for my bed."

Kelly turned around and rested her arms on the wall. "Who needs a bed when you've got my ass?"

Peter stared at the ass like a scientist. "Well, what would I do with it? Rest my head on it?"

"You would fuck it, of course."

Peter gasped. "Fuck it? What's... fuck?"

"Well, first, I can pull my dress down." Kelly started to slip her dress off of her body.

"But Kelly! Then, you'll be naked!"

Kelly was now standing in her panties and bra. It wasn't long before her bra had been thrown to the floor and her ass was bare as well. "Okay, that's step number one."

Peter could swear that he was getting hot flashes.

"Now, you have to at least pull your pants and underwear down."

"But then my privates will be hanging out!"

"Yes! Exactly!"

"Well...I guess I can do that." The naïve man dropped his pants and underwear as planned. Kelly looked at his cock and could see that he was highly aroused, but doubted the man knew exactly what was happening to his cock.

Peter found himself grinning and couldn't figure out why. "Well, I guess that works. What's the next thing that I should do?"

"The next thing that you need to do is to take your cock and slam it right between my ass cheeks."

Peter's eyes widened. "You mean... in there?"

"Yes. And pull it right into my asshole that you will find buried between the two butt cheeks."

Peter took some time to work his cock into the ass cheeks, slowly diving into the asshole without any protection. He didn't really know what protection was anyway. He could tell, however, that as soon as he pulled his cock into the ass, something felt right. "God, wow... that feels pretty good. What should we do next?"

Kelly laughed. "You push it in and out, silly."

"Um, okay, but something reminds me of

how my family told me doing stuff like that would put my eyes out." Peter started to push the cock inside of Kelly. The motion was simple but rough. In and out, in and out. "Mmmm, damn. That feels good."

"Doesn't it?"

Peter was getting rougher in Kelly's ass. It felt really good for both of them. Kelly fingered herself ferociously as her lover fucked her. In and out, his cock fucked her asshole hard. Kelly was moaning, pressed against the wall. Her pussy was dripping down her fingers and hands as she was getting fucked, her ass pressed against the head of Peter's cock like a pillow. She felt like he could go as deep as he wanted to. In time, her moans were filling his entire house. Before long, her legs were trembling, her ass gripped against the cock with friction as he dug.

Peter hugged Kelly's ass tight with his hands. At first, the sensations he was feeling seemed so distant from anything he had ever experienced before. He was a quick learner though. The feeling of her ass encouraged his big cock to take risks inside of her, dipping inside of her like a swordfish. He tried to hit her ass with force, pressed against her harder and harder. Her moans and screaming pleased him. At first, he thought he was hurting her, but then he realized that he was doing everything right because she kept saying, "More." At times, she would say it under her breath, and later, she was screaming it. "More, more, more!"

He delivered, as she demanded. His cock

fucked deep inside of her. One of his hands even took the liberty of spanking her. He felt some creativity in that. He wanted to be a little different with each approach. He fingered her deeply, fucking Kelly as she screamed and felt his dick throbbing. Harder, harder, harder... He didn't know how long he had been in her.

Suddenly, he felt something oozing out of his dick. He didn't know what it was, but it felt good. Kelly held her ass out with a smile as she felt him leak inside of her.

As Peter panted loudly, he pulled out of Kelly. He was catching his breath as she watched the beauty pick up her clothes, starting to get dressed.

"So, Kelly," the man said with heavy pants, "when can we meet again?"

"Can't, sorry," Kelly said honestly. "Back to the drawing board."

AUTHOR'S NOTE

Readers: I want to expand a few of the stories to see where the characters can be explored further. If there are any of the stories that you would like to read more about again, I'd love to hear from you!

Visit my blog at www.parkerheimann.com

Join my newsletter for free exclusive previews
http://www.parkerheimann.com/in

Follow me on Twitter at
http://www.twitter.com/parkerheimann

Like my page on Facebook at
http://www.facebook.com/parkerheimann

Discover my books at major ebook retailers everywhere.